CIPHER

INTERGALACTIC DATING AGENCY

DRAGON BRIDES
BOOK 4

KATE RUDOLPH

Published by Kate Rudolph.
www.katerudolph.net

ABOUT CIPHER

Cipher needs a bride if he wants to keep his inheritance...

When an ultimatum sets Cipher on a path to find his bride, his first stop is the Royal Matchmaker. But Cipher doesn't want just any woman. He needs a perfect lady dragon who can handle all that society has to throw at her. A human with a checkered past will never do.

Not even when he's certain that she's his fated mate.

Morgan just needs a way home...

Ditched on a deserted planet, Morgan is losing hope of ever escaping. When a gorgeous alien crash lands on the planet, that hope comes roaring back. Maybe he has a way off the planet.

Or maybe they can just cuddle for warmth.

With Cipher at her side, she just might stand a

chance against all the planet can throw at them. But the dragon is blowing hot and cold. And no matter how much her body burns for his, she refuses to give her heart to a man who doesn't think she's good enough for him.

But what fate has brought together, no challenge can tear apart.

And when Cipher sets his mind to wooing Morgan for real, she doesn't stand a chance at resisting him.

PROLOGUE

CIPHER SAT in his mother's salon with a growing sense of doom burbling in his gut. He was an adult, the oldest of her three children, and for some reason he still feared that she would send him to his quarters in shame for some mischief he and his brothers had done.

He eyed Storm and Drake, who sat on either side of him. Drake looked pleasant as always, while Storm lived up to his name, danger brewing in his gaze. He hadn't seen his brothers in weeks, each of them sent to far reaches of the planet on their mother's business.

They hadn't done anything wrong.

That didn't convince his nerves of anything.

A servant opened the door and their mother glided in. She was nearly as tall as her three sons, an icy, elegant woman who could make weaker debutantes cry with a single raised eyebrow. And she surveyed Cipher and his brothers like she was preparing to send them to war.

She settled in behind her desk and Cipher's dread bloomed. She was up to something. She always had her little plots and schemes, often playing him and his brothers against one another until she got exactly what she wanted. They'd learned to outwit her, or at least outrun her since they'd become adults.

But she knew their tricks even better than they knew hers.

"I've accepted an assignment from King Venin," she announced. She was always careful to give his majesty his due, even in private. He was never *my brother* or *your uncle*, but always the king.

Neither he nor his brothers asked questions. Any interest could be a weakness, and they wouldn't open themselves up to exploit this quickly.

Her gaze raked over them, fire banked deep in her amber eyes. "I'm set to represent the king and his government as the governor of a new dragon colony. I've agreed to one year. The three of you will be responsible for managing my affairs while I'm away."

Cipher took a deeper breath than he should have and was caught in his mother's gaze. But he could handle it. It meant she didn't notice Storm flinch.

She let the announcement hang for a long moment before continuing. "It's long past time I've named my heir. You have until I return to prove your worth. And I will not play games with our legacy. If you are not wed to suitable matches by the time I return, you'll be disqualified. I've arranged meetings with the matchmaker for all of you. Don't disappoint me."

He could feel the heat of those words, even though she kept her fire tightly banked.

"Mother!" Drake objected, nearly coming out of his seat in outrage.

Cipher sighed. He did his best to protect his brothers, but he couldn't help them if they called down their mother's fury on themselves.

He let the condition roll around his mind while his mother laid out, in no uncertain terms, exactly what she expected of them in the next year. Cipher had never given his heart to another, had never seen a reason.

If he were honest, which was a dangerous thought in his mother's salon, he'd been hoping he'd find his mate.

He was a fool. Fated mates were a gift from the stars and rare enough that waiting for one was absurd.

And yet, his three royal cousins had all found their mates. Two of them with humans, no less. The news had first rocked all of the dragon kingdom, but as the newest dragon brides had settled into their roles, they'd proved to all that they cared for their new land.

But Cipher had to let the dream of his mate go.

Finding a woman his mother approved of would be difficult enough. Hoping she was his fated mate was an impossible wish he could not afford to keep.

THE END of the meeting with his mother put him in a sour mood, and the only way Cipher could clear his head was to take to the skies and fly. The people on the ground were barely specks at his altitude and he enjoyed the quiet.

Few dragons dared to fly so high. The air was thinner, harder to control, and if he stayed too long, even his thick hide would begin to feel the bite of the cold.

Would his chosen bride fly so high with him?

He let out a burst of flame and swooped low as a wave of injustice threatened to send him spiraling to the ground. He should be allowed to choose his own woman, to find his own mate. Instead, he had a meeting with a matchmaker and instructions to find a woman his mother would like.

Ha! His mother didn't even like her own children.

She was more than likely to reject any bride and hold their inheritances over their heads until her dying day. And then she'd hurt them one last time when her final wishes were read.

If he was a better older brother, he would have waited at home to discuss things with Storm and Drake. Presenting a united front was the only way they had of not bowing to their mother's will.

But this time Cipher didn't see a way out. He was thirty-six years old. Every year the debutantes got younger, and the thought of wedding one made him faintly ill. There had to be at least one dragoness closer to his age with whom he could make a life.

He dove again, this time shifting at the final second and landing on human feet.

He was on the edge of the city and had his appointment with the matchmaker in half an hour. Cipher was so tempted to skip it that he nearly leapt back into the air to fly home. But his mother was still at the estate for another day, and running into her was even worse than speaking with the matchmaker.

Besides, he didn't need to act on whatever he heard. He'd listen politely, see if any prospects would be suitable, and, if not, go on his way and find a woman he could tolerate through his own means.

He walked with the kind of determination that made other pedestrians dodge out of his way. To Cipher, they may as well have not existed.

The sign outside of his destination was discreet: *Royal Matchmaker* written in a flowing script with a smaller sign that indicated the business was open. Cipher could still walk away. But he summoned his will and opened the door, stepping inside as if he was about to go into battle.

But he'd never battled in a cozy tea shop.

He looked back at the door to make sure he was in the right place. He wasn't sure what he expected of the Royal Matchmaker, but definitely not two comfortable, patterned sofas, a low table, and a tea pot with two delicate cups on a tray beside a small plate of cookies.

A middle-aged woman with light brown skin, dark hair, and striking blue eyes walked out from behind a curtain, a polite smile on her face. "Good afternoon, sir. May I help you?"

He'd heard rumors this woman was psychic. Perhaps, if he was willing to trust her, she could point him to his mate.

If such a woman existed.

But the idea of revealing his deepest desires made him faintly ill. There was a better than even chance that every word he said would be repeated back to his mother or one of her agents. He'd have to watch his tongue.

"I have an appointment," he said, the words harsher than was polite.

"Your name?" She pulled out a leatherbound note-book from a small desk and flipped it open.

"Cipher." He forced himself to modulate his voice. This woman wasn't his mother and was only doing her job. She deserved a bare minimum amount of courtesy. It was his duty to set an example for others, and he would not become some tyrant simply because he was in a bad mood.

The woman consulted her book before making a small notation, closing it, and putting it back in its drawer. "My lord, welcome. My name is Shade and I look forward to working with you. Please," she said, gesturing to the sofas. "Have a seat."

If he sat, this might take more than a handful of minutes. Of course, he'd been kidding himself if he ever thought it might end before the tea was drunk. Perhaps she had some sort of ritual that he had to endure before she brought out the list of prospective brides.

He took his seat and noticed a small stack of fliers neatly placed at the edge of the table, one for a service called the Intergalactic Dating Agency. He had to bite his lip to keep from scoffing. He could deal with a matchmaker, but he wouldn't be contacting anyone else, certainly not an *agency*.

Shade poured their tea and took two dainty cookies for herself. For a moment Cipher thought he'd resist the sweets out of spite, but the cookies hadn't done anything to hurt anyone. They deserved to be eaten. He smiled faintly at his own absurdity as he nibbled.

"The fact that your mother is forcing your hand makes you hostile to me," Shade said between sips. "And yet you still came. Interesting."

"Forcing my hand?" He couldn't stop himself from responding, and he wondered if the tea was loosening his tongue. Cipher put his cup down, but managed not to glare at it.

"I haven't drugged you, my lord. I am merely observant." She poured more tea into her own cup and pointedly filled his back up.

"I heard you're more than observant." Rumors swirled through the city faster than anything else, and Cipher made it his business to know what was important. He'd mostly ignored anything he heard about the matchmaker, but after her name became closely associated with the princes and their mates, he'd done a little research.

It paid to be prepared.

Shade merely shrugged. "There are three dragons you will find acceptable on the planet. Your mother will find two of those women acceptable. You *may* be able to make a love match with one of them."

This didn't sound like psychic predictions, but it was what he was here for. "I'm sure you have dossiers. Will you set up meetings with the two acceptable women?" The third one intrigued him, but he wouldn't sacrifice his inheritance for an arranged match his mother wouldn't like.

Shade nibbled on another cookie and stared at him, her eyes getting a far off look in them after a moment. "You want me to tell you about your mate."

Despite himself, he leaned in closer. He hadn't said a word to anyone about wanting a true mate. But it didn't make Shade psychic to know he might want one. Who wouldn't? But he forced himself not to ask. He was giving up that dream.

Shade didn't make him say a word. "If you want to meet your mate, you must take a journey. You will not find her among the suitable brides on this planet."

"She exists?" He meant to scoff, meant to dismiss her words and demand she set up the meetings he should be having. Instead, he needed to know more. "When? Where? What is she like?"

But Shade only shook her head. "Fate does not like intervention. I may merely set things into motion, and only with a gentle hand. Saying anything else would do more harm than good."

That sounded like something a fraudulent psychic would say. It was impossible to be wrong when a woman refused to make predictions.

Cipher got up from the couch and stomped towards the door. "We're done here."

Shade stood as if he wasn't throwing a temper

tantrum and crossed the room to shake his hand. "I shall prepare the dossiers on your prospective brides. You may pick them up next week. Unless you take your journey." She opened the door for him.

The sounds from the street broke a bit of the spell he hadn't realized he'd been under. Cipher wanted to tell her to keep her dossiers—he'd find a bride himself—but he bit his tongue. He was on a deadline and had no luck at wooing eligible women, at least not for more than a bit of fun and flirtation.

But as he stalked through the streets to the edge of town, where he could launch himself into the sky and fly home, he couldn't help but think of the other possibility.

His mate was out there—if he was brave enough to take a journey. He pumped his wings faster, eager to get home.

He had to pack.

"I BRING YOU *FIRE!*" Morgan Murphy watched as smoke billowed up in a tiny stream, stronger and stronger as she heard a crackle. "Ha! Take that Bart, I'm not dead yet." She blew on her tiny flame and watched as yellow overtook the gray smoke. It wasn't her first successful campfire, but it was the fastest.

After fourteen days, she was starting to get the hang of this.

She had a trio of small fish hanging from a hook she'd fashioned on a small rock face. She'd managed to find enough branches and leaves to make something that almost resembled a tent and did an okay job at blocking the wind and rain. Her bones ached with the chill and every day seemed colder than the last.

But she was still alive.

She just didn't know how much longer she'd manage to stay that way.

"No, no, no!" She watched as the flames sputtered out. She hovered over her creation, adding a few dry leaves and blowing on the whole pile until the smoke started back up and the fire came back to life. Morgan stared at it this time, until she was sure it was big enough not to die.

Then she grabbed the fish and shuddered. Luckily, she'd had a knife on her when Bart threw her off the ship. Otherwise, she'd be trying to butcher fish with her bare hands. And it was gross enough with the knife.

If she had a functioning communicator or information tablet, she might be brave enough to eat some of the few plants she'd found growing on this barren rock. But she didn't know what was poison and had no access to medical care.

But she was pretty sure the meat was safe.

She hoped.

Who ever got poisoned by meat so long as it was cooked enough?

"Is fish technically meat?" She'd started talking to herself in the hours after the ship took off and she hadn't stopped. She was all alone, and she might go crazy if she stayed silent.

Though, if she were honest, she'd admit that the whole talking to herself thing wasn't anything new. It got lonely in the engine room. But down there, she was talking to her machines. And sometimes they answered.

Okay. Maybe she was going crazy.

She got some meat off her fish and set it up on her makeshift pan on the fire. It was a piece of metal she'd scavenged from an old vehicle that looked like it had crashed decades before. There were no permanent settlements on this little rock, but she'd found plenty of evidence of exploration. A couple downed ships, some old vehicles, even an old hut she'd spent two nights in before moving on.

That detritus gave her hope. The planet wasn't exactly out of the way and ships had clearly used it as a stopover before. Maybe one of them would stop and she'd get a ride home.

Of course, she didn't have credits to pay for it. But that was a problem for another time.

She ate the fish as soon as it was cooked, wincing at the heat on her tongue. It was best to eat it hot. She had no spices, no way to cover the oily, slightly bitter taste of this pink and green fish that teemed in the nearby river. But the heat made it almost taste okay.

She might actually kill someone for a burger.

No. Morgan couldn't think of a juicy burger, cheese melting off the edges, the bun toasted to perfection and the toppings perfectly complementing the meat.

She forced another piece of fish down and

grimaced. Definitely not as good as one of the burgers from Lenny's Diner back on the space station. Of course, if she headed back there, Bart might actually kill her.

He'd say she deserved it, but he was a dirty slaver, and she didn't regret a thing. Except that she'd worked for him for six months without realizing he was running errands for some of the biggest slave outfitters in this chunk of the galaxy.

If she managed to get off this rock and find another crew, she was asking a *lot* more questions before she agreed to work for them. She was happy to work for mercs or other crews with a variety of shady dealings, but she drew the line at slavery.

She was almost glad Bart hadn't paid her out for the last six months of work. That was blood money and she shouldn't touch it.

But planning her next move might be a bit easier if she had credits she could work with.

"One thing at a time," she muttered. "You've gotta get off this place before you worry about money." That was one perk to being stranded on a deserted planet. She hadn't spent a single credit. Couldn't spend money when there weren't any shops.

She ate more fish.

She heard something like a roaring crash of thunder and looked up to see fire streaking through the sky. Morgan dove for cover, but the fireball moved west of her. A minute later, she heard the boom of a crash.

That was a ship. A personal vehicle by the size of the fire, could probably hold a crew of up to eight. A ship that size would have an automech rather than waste the space on an extra crew member.

And they could be in trouble.

Entering an atmosphere was always a fiery event, but the fire was supposed to stop long before a ship hit the ground. That one hadn't landed so much as crashed. Unfortunately, that meant she wasn't getting off the planet any sooner.

But there could be survivors. They could need help. And they could have the means to call for it.

Morgan stuffed the rest of the fish in her mouth and swallowed it down with water from her canteen. Then she gave her pitiful fire a look before dousing it and making sure it was out all the way before she left. Things were bad enough, she wasn't going to start a wildfire because of poor fire safety.

She found her flashlight and stuck it in her utility belt before making her way towards where she thought the ship had crashed down.

Maybe she was about to find her way off of this rock after all.

CHAPTER
THREE

THE GROUND SHIFTED under Cipher as he groggily rose to consciousness. His entire body ached and his mouth tasted like ash. Gravity was a heavy weight, and he knew something was wrong.

He wasn't on his ship.

His last memory was warning lights blaring as the safety system announced a full system shut down. Then everything went black.

He lay on something metal which bumped over rocks and dirt. Whoever was pulling him cursed in a feminine voice. It almost made him smile. But he wouldn't be charmed by a few foul words from a pretty tongue.

Careful not to give away that he was awake, he let his eyes drift half open so he could see his surroundings. Brown rock. Pathetic, droopy trees. Murky sky in the distance. It looked like it was dusk, but one never knew on new planets.

His captor—or rescuer if he was willing to give her the benefit of the doubt—paused, and the sled carrying him came to a stop. Cipher couldn't afford to trust her, not when he doubted that his mother would pay a hefty ransom.

He summoned his flame as he leapt up, firing beside his captor just in case she hadn't actually meant him harm. If she shot at him, then he'd turn lethal.

She screamed, and somehow his flame grew in a burst before dying out as if it had never been there. Cipher's eyes widened, and he was so shocked that he didn't immediately summon more fire.

Had this woman controlled his flame?

This *human?*

Now that he was standing, a sled made of scavenged parts of his own ship between them, he got a good look at her. Her face was gaunt, as if she'd been living hard for some time. Her dark hair looked as if she'd chopped it off with a knife, far from the stylish quaffs he saw back home. Her skin was red and peeling in places, and he knew it should have been much paler and creamy. Humans and dragons looked quite alike, after all. But in certain suns, humans burned.

She was short and small, perfect for hiding in little crevasses and attacking the unsuspecting. Was that what she did? Did she kidnap wary travelers and extract ransom? Or worse?

Whatever this planet was, she'd chosen a poor place for her scheme. There was no traffic in the space overhead, and he hadn't been hailed by anyone on the ground. This place was deserted.

"Holy crap!" she finally said, wide, dark eyes blinking madly. "I could have used you these past weeks. You can shoot fire?" She moved her hand in front of her as if *she* were the one controlling his flame.

Was she alright? Perhaps she was alone on this planet because there was something very wrong with her. But Cipher couldn't stop himself from showing off a little. It was nice to be appreciated. "Dragon," he explained, summoning a puff of smoke and a bloom of fire.

She stared at the flame as it died, then pointed to herself. "Morgan. Nice to meet you, Dragon. And you're welcome. What the hell?" She stalked forward two steps before freezing and looking at his hands, probably remembering the fire. Then she backed up again.

This had to be the strangest encounter of his life. "My name isn't Dragon. I *am* a dragon. And I'm called Cipher." To show he could be gracious, he bowed. "Thank you for the rescue. And I apologize for my reaction. I was unsure of your intentions." He still was, honestly.

Morgan narrowed her eyes, but shrugged after a moment. "I've had worse. So dragons exist? For real? You look like a guy." She crouched down and piled a few fallen items back onto the cart. He must have disrupted them when he stood.

"Are those my survival packs? You can't just take my things!" He was a dragon lord. There were laws. King Venin would throw any peasant who dared steal from him into the dungeon.

But they were far outside of King Venin's territory.

Morgan stood, crossed her arms, and glared at him. "Do you know how unstable a crashed ship is? The FTL drive alone could incinerate anything within a kilometer if it blows. We need to give it a bit of time to cool off before we check for anything. I grabbed what I could, including *you*, and hauled ass." She grabbed for one of the packs. "You know what? Fine. I'm taking one survival pack for my troubles. The sled is yours. Good luck surviving." She took a few steps before turning back. "If someone does come for you, can you at least mention that I'm here and need a ride?"

She started walking again, and Cipher had to chase after her. "Wait!" he said. "Please, wait!"

She stopped, but said nothing.

"I apologize again. I have a habit of saying everything wrong." No need to add that it rarely mattered. Who was going to reprimand him back home? "Don't go." This woman had some knowledge of the planet, he'd be a fool to let her walk away.

And she might have controlled his flame.

The matchmaker had told him to take a journey. Was it possible he'd found his mate so soon? Of course, his mother would never accept a human. But he wasn't sure he cared.

Cipher wasn't about to make any drastic decisions yet. But he couldn't let this woman get away.

"Whatever," Morgan finally said. "I guess you can help light the fire. Come on. You can push the sled."

The sled. Right. Cipher wasn't completely useless. Sure, back home he had a fleet of servants to take care of the manual labor, but he'd done his time in the military and could haul heavy things with the best of them. The fact that it took him a solid minute to get it moving since one corner got stuck in the dirt was something best kept to himself.

He followed Morgan and was shocked at how fast she moved. His legs were quite a bit longer than hers, and yet he had to work to keep up. Of course, he was maneuvering a heavy sled.

She didn't talk to him anymore, though he could have sworn he heard whispers. Was she talking to herself? "How long have you been here?" he asked. What if she'd grown up here? Was he the first person she'd ever seen?

No. That was absurd.

"About fourteen days. Two Earth weeks. My old crew dumped me here, the turds." She didn't elaborate on why.

Cipher wanted to ask, but something caught his attention. It wasn't a sound, not exactly. It was the *lack* of it. The planet might not have had spacefaring life forms, but it teemed with activity, and as they'd walked, he'd been listening to the sounds of insects and birds chirping.

Now there was nothing.

"Stop moving," he said as quietly as he could. "Don't speak."

Morgan gave him a sharp look, but something on his face must have imparted how serious he was. She stilled and stayed quiet.

Cipher let his flame rise to the surface but didn't summon it. If he had room he would have shifted to his other form, but they were in a small pass and he wasn't sure he could fit.

The perfect place for an ambush.

Had Morgan led him into one?

No. If she had, she'd already be running. She didn't strike him as the shifty type. Whatever threat they were facing, it came from the planet itself.

The shadows were growing longer as night crept up on them. And one of the shadows under a dry bush moved towards them with the liquid motion of a predator. It was roughly the size of one of the sky tigers that lived in the far off mountains back home, though this animal had no wings. Its fur appeared gray, though that could have been due to the low light. And its eyes were red.

Not good.

It roared, fangs dripping something viscous to the ground. And then it charged.

Cipher was between it and Morgan, and he wasn't letting this beast attack the woman, some instinct inside of him insisting she was too important. It couldn't have her, not while he lived.

He shot a stream of fire towards it, but didn't connect. The beast reared back before dodging to the side and trying to get around it.

Cipher kept the fire going and the beast couldn't get any closer. But it roared again, this time even angrier.

"We're in its territory," Morgan shouted at him. "Maybe he won't follow us if we leave. Come on." He heard the sled move behind him as she grabbed it, but she didn't start moving.

"What are you doing?" he demanded. He could keep the fire up for a long time, but not forever.

She opened one of the packs and pulled out a block of protein clay. It was as unappetizing as it sounded, but it could keep most species alive for quite some time.

Morgan chucked it towards the beast. "Maybe he'll

eat that instead of us." She sealed up the bag and pulled the sled.

Cipher pulled in his fire close enough to protect them, no longer the huge blanket of flame that kept the beast from moving at all. And he was careful not to incinerate the protein clay.

They moved slowly, though his instincts beat at him to run, shift, and pick up Morgan before the beast could get to them. It could never take a dragon in his sky form. But running prey would be an irresistible temptation for the beast.

Once they were clear of the narrow passage, Cipher let go of his flame. No need to waste it just yet. And there was still enough sunlight to see by.

The beast didn't follow them any further.

But Cipher would keep the threat in mind.

"Come on," Morgan said, voice surprisingly steady. "That thing hasn't bothered me where I've been sleeping. We need to hurry. We have to cross a stream, and getting this crap over it is going to be difficult enough. I want to get there before full dark."

MORGAN WAS LIMPING by the time they got the last survival pack across the stream. Cipher took one look at her fire pit and started the fire with a thought.

"Must be nice," she muttered. Then she clamped her mouth shut, remembering a moment too late that he could hear her. She wasn't alone anymore. She had to put on her people manners.

It was easier hanging out with machines.

She sank down onto the most comfortable rock she could find, and somehow that only made her feet hurt worse. She hadn't been on the planet long enough to form the callouses she'd need to survive.

Cipher was stacking the survival packs far away from the fire, but she must have made a sound. His head snapped her way. "Are you injured?"

Morgan groaned and tried not to whimper. She'd stayed close to her hut and the stream for the past few days, and she'd forgotten how bad it felt to walk long distances. "It's my feet," she said. "I think a blister or two might have popped. Do you have healing cream in one of those bags?" She hadn't checked to see if any of the survival packs were specifically marked for first aid, but basic healing supplies were pretty standard.

Cipher checked the nearest bag and came back with a small blue tube. "Here's some regen gel."

Her eyes widened, and she wanted to grab the tube and clutch it close. Regen gel was freaking magical. It could heal the worst of wounds in a matter of hours or days. Even broken bones. "Don't waste that on my feet. Really, just a bit of healing cream will be fine. Or even a water bath."

Regen gel also cost a king's ransom. Bart refused to buy it for the crew. Back home her mom had used her supply so sparingly that Morgan couldn't remember her ever needing to resupply. And here was Cipher just handing over something that cost at least hundreds of credits like it was nothing.

Who was this guy?

"There's likely more," he said dismissively and sat down beside her. "Now what's wrong? We have the gel so we might as well use it. Or do you want it to go to waste?"

There was something off about that logic, but she

couldn't quite tell, what with pain radiating up into her ankles. "Fine," she relented. She wasn't about to martyr herself. "Hand it over."

"Which foot?" he asked instead. His hand hovered over her legs.

"Both of them. I walked them bloody my first day here, and they haven't had a chance to heal. I think one might be infected." She hadn't wanted to admit it to herself. It was impossible to keep her feet clean with what she had, though she washed them as often as possible. She had no access to medical care. An infection could kill her.

"Let me tend you," Cipher said, and somehow made it sound like she was doing him a favor. "After all, you did save my life."

She put her left foot on his lap. It would be easier for him to treat her.

"What kind of boots are these?" He was aghast as he undid the laces and slid them off.

She laughed at his tone. She'd gotten used to the minor horrors of her situation and his reaction was almost funny. "I didn't exactly realize I was leaving the ship for good," she said. "Bart dumped me planetside with nothing but a canteen and the clothes on my back." She wiggled her toes, and Cipher obligingly slathered them in regen gel.

Morgan moaned as the cool gel immediately began

to relieve some of the pain. Oh yeah, that was good. No wonder people paid so much for this stuff.

"Who's Bart?" Cipher asked. He was gentle as he applied the gel to the worst of her cuts and blisters. "And what does that have to do with your appalling shoes?"

"It didn't matter that my boots were too big on the ship. They belonged to the previous mechanic before Bart fired him. I got his stuff." Then something occurred to her. "That dick is going to give my stuff to the new mechanic!" She sighed. Nothing to be done about it now. Maybe it should have been a warning sign when she was hired.

"The boots are great for maneuvering around an engine room. Not so great for trudging on a planet. They're heavy and inflexible. Half the time I've been going around barefoot since it hurts less. I only wore them because I knew I'd likely be going through debris at the crash site." He wrapped her foot up in gauze he must have also taken from a survival pack and shifted feet.

"Who's Bart?" Cipher asked again. He was tending to her feet with the kind of intensity she'd seen from mercs heading into war zones.

"He's the scum of the earth masquerading as my old boss. Seriously, if I had your fire powers, I'd fry him to a crisp." For some reason, Cipher smiled at that. "What?" she asked. "You're never tempted to barbecue people? What kind of dragon are you?"

"I'm afraid that humans have very distorted ideas of who and what dragons are. But perhaps you are right about this Bart creature. Tell me more." He slathered regen gel on a particularly nasty blister.

Morgan winced. Right. Bart. "I was looking for a job. He was hiring. Really good pay. Not a lot of info about the jobs he took. I thought it didn't matter. I was just tending to the ship, you know. Not like I was doing anything to hurt people."

His grip on her foot tightened for a moment before he loosened it. He didn't say anything.

It made Morgan sick to think of what she'd found. And she felt beyond stupid. Of course Bart was dirty. Clean mercs couldn't pay that well. "Anyway, I was with the crew for a few months. And, yeah, there were some red flags that I ignored. But I figured I hadn't actually *seen* anything too bad. We weren't transporting slaves. I'd have been gone at the first whiff of that. And I made it clear to Bart that I wouldn't work with slavers before I signed on. He promised that he didn't move people. He *promised*." Rage washed over her, and she had to take a few breaths.

Cipher had finished applying the regen gel, and though he'd bandaged her second foot, he hadn't let go. His green eyes had an eerie glow in the fire's light. He looked like a warrior of old, broad and dour, with dark hair that should have been held back in a Viking's braids.

He'd make a good barbarian.

And she was stalling.

She forced herself to keep talking. "I found a stash of control chips while I was looking through our supplies. Bart hadn't lied. We didn't move people. We just moved other stuff that slavers need. And I was part of it for nearly six months. I can't believe I was so stupid. Bart caught me, we got into a huge argument. And then he dumped me here. I'm probably lucky he didn't kill me." The rage in his eyes when he realized she'd poured acid over the chips had made her certain she was about to die.

Maybe she'd deserved it. How much misery had she contributed to in those six months? How many people had been stolen because of her?

Those chips robbed people of their will and made them little more than machines made of meat. She'd rather die than be controlled like that.

Cipher put her foot back on the ground and turned to face the fire. He wiped his hands on a cleaning cloth he must have also taken from his survival pack. "Your feet should be fully healed by morning. Stay still for half an hour or so to give the gel time to set." His tone was brusque, bordering on chilly.

Was it something she'd said?

Morgan opened her mouth to say something, she

wasn't sure what, but Cipher stood and went back to looking through the survival packs, acting as if she weren't there at all.

And, to think, she'd been starting to like the guy! Maybe she was an easy date; a foot massage and a nice fire and she was nearly ready to see how warm they could make each other. But that wasn't going to happen if he kept running hot and cold.

Morgan stared into the fire and watched as some of the twigs snapped in the heat. Cipher might be her ride off this planet. No matter how he was acting, she had to keep him close.

CIPHER HAD NEVER BEEN MORE aware of another person his entire life. Tending to Morgan's feet had made him angry. How had she let things get so bad before she let him treat her? It didn't matter that in reality she'd let him treat her the moment it was possible. He could imagine some fantasy scenario where she found an abandoned tub of regen gel and saw to herself.

But then he wouldn't have been the one to help her.

Which was for the best.

He dug through the survival packs, looking for food, and wondered who had put them together. He had enough first aid supplies to tend an army. He'd found an entire mattress rolled up in one of the bags.

But he'd only found two liters of water and four protein bars.

Maybe they shouldn't have thrown the block of protein at the not-sky-tiger.

He had to get off this planet before his instincts got the best of his senses. Morgan was a former *slaver,* or at least a slaver's accomplice. She couldn't be trusted. Yes, he'd heard the anger and sadness in her voice as she told her tale, but how could a person work besides slavers for months and not notice a thing?

That was a pile of dung. Stinking dung. She'd concocted the story that sounded best and would make him sympathize with her. He'd heard enough false sad stories in his life that he could spot one at ten paces.

Then why did she say she was a slaver at all? Some voice in the back of his mind that might have been his conscience dared to ask.

He dug harder through the packs, accidentally tearing one as he moved it aside.

This would all be fine if she had no effect on him. Even if she were the worst kind of person, he owed her a debt for pulling him out of his ship. Things must have been bad if he'd passed out. And she had a point about crashed ships being unstable. It didn't happen often, but when compromised ships blew, the damage was catastrophic.

The fact that they hadn't heard a boom in the night suggested the ship was stable enough. He was tempted to take off and go search through the wreckage without another word to Morgan. She'd saved him from the ship—while stealing his supplies! He'd saved her from that beast—while losing *more* supplies.

They were even.

And yet, he couldn't make his feet move.

She was a fierce, clever little woman and he wanted to find out more. He wanted to strip away the layers of her until he knew her down to the bone. And he wanted to strip her other layers too and find out just what she was hiding under her ill-fitting gray outfit.

He was a dragon, with a dragon's appetites. The urge to take and pillage and plunder burned fiercely within him, and he'd listened to the ancient draconic legends with eager ears as a child. He may have played the civilized lord, but he had his own beast lurking inside.

But he didn't just want to take Morgan and the pleasure it would give to both of them.

She'd affected his flame.

The more he thought about it, the more certain he was it must be true. And more of those ancient stories came rearing back. True dragon mates were not harmed by one another's fire. They could control their mate's flame and direct it as necessary. He'd heard whispers that human mates could even *summon* their mate's fire when the need arose.

But human mates were rare, no matter what had happened to his cousins.

Had Morgan directed his fire? Or had he simply been distracted in the moment?

He could find out right now. All he had to do was shoot fire and ask Morgan to do anything. If she couldn't, it would all be clear.

No mate.

And that was a *good* thing, he had to remind the disappointment trying to sour in him. If he wanted his inheritance, he needed a spouse that his mother would approve of. And she'd never approve of some human who'd been thrown away by her crew of slavers.

Would he really throw away a mate for his mother's approval?

Smoke tickled his nose, and Cipher had to take several deep breaths to get his emotions under control. He wouldn't summon flame without thinking about it, but smoke could happen when his emotions were riled. Which thinking of his mother often did.

His mother had spent her life ruling his. Where he'd gone to school, who he'd been instructed to befriend, even his first lover had been pointed out to him at one of his mother's soirees. He'd spent the last several years trying to untangle himself from her machinations, but with one challenge thrown, he was right back where he'd been a decade ago.

Whoever his mother named would have control of the family. They'd be able to direct their considerable wealth and resources into shaping the kingdom. He'd always assumed the position would be his. Barring extreme circumstances, the eldest inherited the title. His mother had inherited from her mother, his grand-mother from her father, and so on for centuries.

And now his mother was throwing it all into chaos.

If Morgan, or some other unsuitable woman, really was his fated mate, would he walk away? *Could* he?

He looked over to where Morgan had a clutch of dead fish she was butchering with utter incompetence. She had to be wasting half the meat. He'd never butchered a fish in his life, but he was certain he could do better.

Despite the scene, a smile threatened. Her face was a mask of concentration, her tongue sticking out and her nose scrunched up, eyes narrowed as if she thought her bounty might spring back to life and make a break for the stream.

A fated mate was a gift.

But he couldn't be certain that Morgan had redirected his flame. And he could never give his heart to a slaver.

He went back to shuffling through the packs. He needed to find something of use, and then he needed to go home and leave this barren world behind.

MORGAN WAS GETTING BETTER at butchering her fish. She smiled to herself as she got the meat on her pan and cooked it over the fire that Cipher had kept going all night.

Maybe it wasn't so bad to have a dragon hanging around.

Okay, it was kind of great. Even if he was being a standoffish dick.

All of last night he'd kept his distance, even when she'd offered to share her canteen so he wouldn't be thirsty. Instead he'd spent nearly an hour digging through the survival packs until he found water of his own, two measly bottles he was likely to go through in a day.

Then, before she'd had a chance to see if she could make up a bed for him in her makeshift tent, he'd laid out a blanket outside and told her he was going to sleep.

She was trying to be a good host, and he was making it difficult. So she was done trying. No more mister nice Morgan.

She had enough fish for both of them, but she only offered him his portion when she was done eating, and the look he gave her made her wish she hadn't spent extra time in the stream to get those two extra fish.

But after a minute, he did eat. And she didn't take the look on his face when he tasted the fish personally. That wasn't on her.

"We should go back to your ship," she said as he ate. She had to keep this professional. She'd managed to work with Bart's crew for months, and most of them were legitimately terrible people. Cipher was just kind of rude. She could work with rude.

"I agree," he said. Rude, but sensible. Definitely a man she could work with.

She'd expected to have to fight him on it, for some reason, and couldn't make herself stop talking. Maybe that was just the loneliness of the last two weeks. "I didn't have time to check if your rescue beacon was functioning. If it is, someone may already be en route and *we'll* be off this planet in no time."

She paused, waiting for him to make some

comment about how he'd be leaving alone. But he didn't.

Sensible.

"If it's damaged, maybe there's other communication equipment. Or I might be able to play with the beacon to get it to work." Her fingers itched for her tools, but those were back on Bart's ship. It didn't matter. She could do a lot with her hands.

"Yes, I said I agree," Cipher said again. "I'm ready to leave as soon as you are."

She stood on feet that didn't pain her for the first time since landing on this rock and looked towards her boots with a wince. She'd be a fool to walk through the crash site in her bare feet, but the blisters that had been healed by the regen gel would come back with a vengeance if she walked all across the planet in those boots.

Maybe she could carry the boots and only put them on when they were nearing the debris field?

She must have zoned out, she did that sometimes when dealing with problems. Cipher cleared her throat and pulled her out of it. He shoved a cloth wrapped package into her hands and backed away without a word.

Morgan unwrapped it and stared at a pair of finely made survival boots. They were designed to conform to the feet of the wearer, automatically adjusting the size as needed.

No blisters.

She looked around so she could thank Cipher, but he was pulling on his own boots and had his back to her, clearly a sign he didn't want to talk.

How was she supposed to take this? He'd been silent and cold all morning, but he'd given her boots. Or maybe he was just being sensible again. He probably didn't want to slather her feet in regen gel when they got back.

Once they both had their boots on, they took off. Morgan was tempted to take her makeshift sled in case they could find more goodies to scavenge, but decided against mentioning it. They were hoping to find a beacon or communication equipment, something that would get them off this rock. Scavenging for supplies felt like tempting fate somehow.

As they neared the narrow pass where they'd been attacked the day before, Morgan's heartbeat sped up and she felt a strange warmth in her chest. A glance at Cipher showed he'd summoned fire and held it in his palm, ready to strike.

And he looked different.

"Do you have *claws*?" She only remembered after she asked that she was supposed to be cold and indifferent to him. But how could she ignore that? She definitely would have noticed before.

He looked her way, and she saw his skin had taken on a strange sheen, almost as if he had scales. He had longer teeth, too. When, exactly, did they officially become fangs? Because his teeth were sharp and very bitey. "This is my warrior form," he said, the words only slightly slurred around his big teeth. "In case."

Right. In case.

And he was a dragon. Which she knew. Because of the fire. Why wouldn't he also have secret claws and fangs?

If she asked, would he show her his true dragon form? Or was it rude to ask?

It definitely wasn't cold and indifferent.

The heat rumbled in her chest, and she wondered if it was some strange reflection of the fire that he'd summoned. Maybe the wind was blowing just enough so that she could feel the heat.

She imagined what it would be like to have fire powers of her own and splayed her hand out, trying to picture a flame in her palm. For one crazy second, she thought she actually saw sparks. But it must have been a trick of the light.

Morgan kept moving. She'd passed through this area several times and had only seen the beast once. Maybe it didn't come out during the early hours of the day. She eyed the shadows under the bushes, ready to jump into action if anything moved.

But they made it through the pass without catching sight of the beast, and Morgan let out a long breath, some of her muscles unclenching.

Good. She didn't want to get eaten by that thing. It looked like a freaking tiger! And tigers were cool, but not up close and personal when it looked like they wanted to eat you.

A glance at Cipher showed he'd gotten rid of the fire and was back to his normal, human form. *Was* that his normal form? And was it right to call it human? What if he wanted to be all lizardy and flying in the sky, breathing fire on any living thing in his path?

How big was he in his dragon form?

She had a million questions, but cold and indifferent women didn't ask them. And she scowled at herself for deciding on that path. But she wasn't about to change now, not until Cipher learned some freaking manners.

The evidence of the crash appeared slowly. There were small pieces of exploded glass and metal, burnt bits of grass where things too small to survive had landed. There was more and more debris as they got closer, and then it was all there.

Cipher hissed. "This is worse than I thought."

Morgan didn't have a response. With the smoking ruins and the long dusk, it hadn't seemed so desolate yesterday. Looking at it now, she was unsure of how anyone could survive. But the tracks of her makeshift sled still led out of the debris field, evidence of yesterday's recovery.

"Do you want to see if you can recover any cargo?"

she asked, to be nice. Unless he'd packed his bags in solid metal, there was no way anything had survived.

"Let's just find the beacon. It's a standard model. Bright orange casing. You can't miss it."

Even something as brightly colored as a beacon could be easily missed in the piles of smoking metal around them. But Morgan stepped into the mess anyway.

A blaster shot beamed over her shoulder and she crouched low, unable to dive without being impaled on something sharp and dirty.

"Down!" Cipher yelled at the same moment.

The shots kept coming and Morgan had little cover. That heat was back in her chest and when she dared look, she saw that Cipher had fire in his hands. Their eyes met, and the utter calm in his expression was enough to make her think they might actually survive this thing.

Another shot nearly hit her, sending dirt flying up into her face.

Cipher would cover her. She had to find the beacon. If she didn't, she might as well let whoever was shooting at them take a free shot. This was her last chance to go home.

THE SHOTS WERE COMING from more than one direction. Blasters were usually short range, so their assailants were far away enough to not catch each other in cross fire. If Cipher turned his complete focus to eradicating one, he'd be taken out by another.

They knew what they were doing.

His warrior form could take the hit from a few blaster shots, even blasters modified to be lethal. But it *hurt*, and, more importantly, it broke his concentration. Under any other circumstances he would have let his fire out and burned everything in range.

But Morgan was in range. And so was the beacon.

If Morgan was his mate, his fire couldn't harm her. He would not wager her life on his instincts, though, not yet. Besides, his fire was hot enough to melt even the casing of a beacon. If he did that, this whole mission would be for naught.

Morgan slipped deeper into the wreckage and kept low. Their attackers focused most of their fire on him. Good. He could keep them distracted while he worked to find out who was hunting them.

Did they have a ship? Had they teleported down to the planet from a ship in orbit? Why were they shooting without a warning?

A blaster shot lit up his shoulder as if he'd been singed with another dragon's flame and Cipher cursed. The whys didn't matter right now. He'd keep one of them alive for answers. The rest would pay in their blood.

But that meant Cipher had to move. And he had to trust that Morgan could take care of herself. She'd survived alone on the planet thus far. He had no other choice.

The blasters were coming in heaviest from the north, so Cipher went south and ran as fast as his feet could carry him. If he had a bit more room, he would have shifted. If he could clear the debris field, he would.

Let these assholes fight a dragon.

He found the first human hunkered down behind a boulder, blindly blasting away towards the debris field. He went down before he could realize Cipher was there, one blast of fire enough to do him in. The man was middle-aged, human, with pale skin, thread-bare clothes, and a tattoo on his neck that indicated he'd been arrested for selling slaves.

Morgan's old crew?

Cipher took the weapon from his limp hand and sent a blast of flame west to draw blaster fire away from Morgan. Then he sent another burst east, just to be confusing. He tried to spot Morgan, but she was hidden among the wreckage.

He hoped.

Some small part of him wondered if this was all a scheme to capture a dragon lord. They'd think he would catch a hefty ransom. He wouldn't let them get a credit.

But, no, they were shooting at Morgan, too. These scavengers had come to take from his ship and profit. Perhaps they'd hoped to catch the survivors and sell them on. His ship must have sent out an automatic distress call. It wasn't unlikely for scavengers to chase injured spacefarers down and prey on them.

Or perhaps Morgan's old crew had come back to torment her, and his presence was just an added bonus.

He took out another shooter, but his partner, a woman with messy braids and a dirty gray jumpsuit, took off at a run.

Good. Dragons loved the chase. And maybe now he could get some answers.

CHAPTER
EIGHT

NO ONE HAD EVER SHOT at Morgan before and it was freaking her out. How did soldiers do this?

She flinched as a shot hit the ground at the base of a large piece of debris that was holding up part of the cabin of Cipher's ship. The whole place was unstable and one wrong move was likely to make it all crash down on top of her.

Too bad. The beacon had to be here somewhere, and they were going to use it to get home. This whole unexpected camping trip would be nothing more than a bad memory.

As long as she could find the beacon.

"Aha! Yes!" She was standing on one of the walls. The floor was now the ceiling of the ship, and she'd found the hatch where the beacon should be nestled.

Unfortunately, the hatch had burst open on impact

and she could see wires sticking out of it. Not a good sign. But ships were basically made of wires so they didn't necessarily belong to the beacon.

Her focus on the blaster fire outside fell away as she carefully pried open the hatch. She cursed when she saw the wires coming from the bright orange box of the beacon. The beacons were meant to be visible, even in the most mangled of debris. Indestructible, too.

Unfortunately, this one had taken some damage.

Morgan pulled the beacon out of the hatch, grabbing any extra wires she could. It was possible that the damage was merely superficial and if she could find the manual on switch, she'd be able to send a signal.

The beacon was a rectangle about as long as her forearm and twice as thick. It wasn't very heavy, but it was just big enough that carrying it over a large distance would get awkward very quickly.

The metal had cracked along one of the edges and exposed some of the wiring inside. And, because it was just her luck, the side with the crack was also the side with the manual on switch.

And the switch was mangled beyond belief.

Morgan searched around for tools of any kind. Just because the switch didn't work didn't make things hopeless. Wires led to the switch. It was the wires that sent the signal to the heart of the device. So if she could figure out how to manipulate the wires and send the signal, she'd be good to go.

There weren't any tools. Maybe she'd find some in whatever was left of Cipher's engine room, but there was no telling where that room was anymore. If there weren't people actually shooting at them, she could take her time to do this repair right.

Instead, she wasn't sure she could do this repair at all.

A blaster shot hit near enough that Morgan flinched. Then she pushed it away. Cipher was handling the attackers. She had to do her part.

She sat the beacon down and looked around the area again, this time not specifically looking for tools, but for anything that would do the job.

Her eyes snagged on a thin piece of metal that would be small enough to get into the beacon without destroying it. In a perfect world, it would also have a mini-camera attached so she could look at the inside without opening the machine further, but this world had clearly shown her it was far from perfect.

She worked the metal inside the beacon and thought she was on to something when a shadow crossed her path.

It took her mind a moment to realize the danger, and by then, Bart already had the blaster trained on her.

"You're not dead," was his way of greeting her.

Morgan clutched the beacon close to her chest. If he shot it, there would be no fixing it. The energy from the weapon would completely fry the wiring, and that was if the shot didn't blast it into a thousand pieces.

"You're still a piece of scum." She glared at the blaster. "Put that thing away. You haven't shot me yet, so you're not going to. One wrong move, or shot, and we'll be crushed."

Bart considered her for a moment. He wasn't an ugly man, though his soul was stained with blood. He was in his forties, or maybe his fifties, with graying stubble, dark hair that was going gray around the edges, skin roughened by a faraway sun but gone pale from years in space, and bright blue eyes deep with laugh lines.

He was also short, and when she'd hired onto his ship, Morgan had felt a sense of solidarity. Shorties united against an unfairly tall world. But their height, or lack thereof, was the only thing they had in common.

She wasn't a monster.

He holstered his blaster and raised his hands in a show of peace. "Your friend out there better not kill me."

"He's not my friend." Morgan would have said it even if she and Cipher had spent the night bonding and forming an everlasting connection. The fact that he'd turned cold and they'd barely exchanged words after he'd tended to her made it easier to say.

"That's too bad. I remember your trouble making friends." He actually sounded sympathetic.

And for a moment, Morgan allowed herself to remember the good times on his ship. The camaraderie, the jokes, the listening ear Bart always had for any problem. He was a good captain, did his job well. And used every nugget of information he learned against crew who wanted to leave.

"It's been two weeks, why are you here?" Had this been some plot to soften her up? Morgan didn't want to fool herself. There were plenty of mechs out there who would gladly go along with Bart's business. He didn't need her.

Unless he did.

Because she was the only mech on *this* chunk of rock.

"There's something wrong with your ship." It wasn't a question. Bart was a good captain… socially, but he left necessary repairs to the last minute and she'd spent half the time in the engine room praying things held together between jobs.

If she'd had time, she might have tried to sabotage the ship before he kicked her off, but she hadn't even had time to grab proper boots.

Her toes curled in the boots that Cipher had given her. Maybe they hadn't spoken beyond what was necessary, but he hadn't had to give her the footwear.

"Come back with me," Bart said, holding out a hand. "I'll save you from this rock. Get us to the nearest space station with a halfway decent repair shop and I'll pay out your wages and you can go find another mech gig. I'll even give you a reference. I've got friends."

She scowled, but he plowed on before she could interrupt.

"Friends in different sectors of the business. No people. Clean hands, all that. We can head up now and you'll be out of this sector before nightfall. How does that sound?" He smiled widely and beckoned her out of the wreckage.

And Morgan was tempted. Of course she was. A ship off this planet? Her wages? A new job that had nothing to do with imprisoning and enslaving people? It was too good to be true.

Really, certainly too good to be true.

"Your people started shooting the second we got here. Are Tex and Marie out there? Were they happy with the thought of laying me out? What were you planning? Knock me out and imprison me? Force me to fix the ship?" She glared at him. Tex and Marie had been the two mercs she'd almost call friends. They'd often shared meals together. And then Tex and Marie had stood right by Bart as he abandoned her here.

Some dark emotion passed over Bart's face before he managed to smother it. "We didn't expect the man. Tell me about his tech. How's he making that fire?"

If he didn't know about dragons, Morgan wouldn't tell him. And she noticed he didn't answer her question. With the beacon busted, Bart was her only way off this planet.

But could she really do it? And could she abandon Cipher? Yeah, he was a bit rude, but that didn't mean he should be left to rot.

"Sounds like the blaster shots have stopped," she said. "So I guess his tech is working well. He's going to come find me soon. And I don't think he'll be kind to you." Half of her survival instincts were screaming that she was being an idiot. Bart was giving her a way off this planet. The other half knew Bart couldn't be trusted a single bit.

All of her knew she wasn't abandoning Cipher.

"The offer's open," Bart said, shuffling back out the makeshift entrance. "But wait too long and I'll come find you. My second offer won't be so nice."

Before she could think of some retort, he was gone.

And Morgan was left with a broken beacon and the dread that came from having no good choices.

CIPHER WAS RIDING HIGH on victory. He'd only taken out two of the mercs; the rest had fled before he got to them. But he'd made his point and they'd think again before coming for him. Or Morgan.

He found Morgan on the edge of the debris field, sitting in the open without a care in the world and fiddling with a large orange box.

"Does the concept of taking cover mean nothing to you?" he snapped, the joy of victory fading as he imagined her laid low by a lucky shot.

She looked up from the box and blinked her big eyes at him before glancing towards the ridge where the shooters who'd gotten away had run from. "The shooting stopped several minutes before I left cover. I'm not stupid."

He had choice words waiting on his tongue, and

his whole body threatened to let smoke pour out. But he caged his temper. They were both alive and the enemy had fled. For now, that was a victory.

She worked for another minute before her hand stilled. "Did you kill any of them?" she asked quietly.

And that was confirmation enough that she suspected it was her former crew. "Two," he confirmed. "The bodies 'ported away before I could do more than look at them."

It was a security feature for shadier merc crews. Short range teleporters were expensive, but well worth their cost when they could put a crew in a highly secure zone without leaving a trace. And they were often programmed to teleport bodies before they could be discovered.

She took a deep, steadying breath and nodded. "They were shooting at us. You had to." The words were for him, but she was clearly comforting herself.

Cipher had no sympathy for her old crew. They worked alongside slavers. They were eager to fire on unarmed people. And they'd been mean to Morgan.

But she'd known them. Had worked beside them for months. It was hard when people you knew died.

"We should head back to camp in case they come back." If they'd all teleported off planet, they likely wouldn't return for a while. The energy usage of teleporters was off the charts and they'd want to ration their 'ports.

If the survivors were still on planet, they could be back at any moment.

Morgan shook her head and held up the box. "I'm working on repairing the beacon. Did you find a toolkit in any of the survival packs?" Her expression was optimistic when she looked up from her project.

He did a quick mental inventory before shaking his head. "No. There might have been a small sewing kit, but nothing else."

She let out a stream of curses. "Then we need to camp here for now. Unless… I should have asked this last night. Do you have a personal communicator?" Her face scrunched up in hope.

He hated to dash it. "My comm was in my quarters. It hooks into the ship while in flight, so there's no need to carry it around." He looked out over the wreckage and couldn't begin to guess where his quarters might have been. "I would have mentioned it last night. No need to ask."

"We might need to pick around to find your quarters, see if we can find the comm."

"That dire, huh?" He wanted to sit down next to her and see if they could work through the problem together, but they were too exposed. "We'll keep close to the field, but let's find a place with a bit more cover."

She opened her mouth to say something but closed

it after a moment and nodded. "Can you carry this?" She offered the broken beacon up.

He knew he should be keeping his hands free in case of attack, but for some reason, he couldn't say no. He took the beacon and stumbled a step. It was heavier than expected.

He looked at Morgan with new eyes. She might have been tiny, but she was *strong*. She was hiding muscles under those clothes. Her outfit hung off of her, but it was clean. She'd scavenged it from one of his survival packs. He hadn't noticed at first, but now he couldn't stop looking at her.

If he had her back home, he'd try and drape her in silks. And when she dirtied those up by playing around in any engine room she could find, he'd buy her the sturdiest jumpsuit he could find. His mate deserved the finest things.

He stumbled again, but this time it had nothing to do with the beacon.

Morgan shot him a concerned look. "I can take it, if you need me to," she offered.

"I'm fine." It came out more harshly than intended, but he was a dragon lord and he wouldn't be insulted.

He purposefully looked away from Morgan and scouted for a better resting place, one that gave them cover but wouldn't leave them pinned. Looking away from her didn't help, though. Her image was imprinted on his mind.

How would she look in a gown at a royal presentation ball? Would she chafe and run away? Or was she hiding a lady underneath the grease? She had the survival instincts of a dragon, that was for certain. And though dragons liked to dress up and dance and act civilized, they all wore predators as their second skin.

It wouldn't matter if she didn't fit in at a ball. Dragons respected survivors.

And so long as she was in his bed, he didn't care if others approved of her. Not when she belonged to him.

The more he thought of it, the more certain he was that she had affected his flame. He wasn't some green dragonling to lose control of his own fire. And he wouldn't let his mother dictate his life like this.

If Morgan was his mate, he intended to have her. Who was he to argue with fate?

He wanted her settled under cover so that he could keep her safe and close. There weren't many options, but he settled on a slight overhang that shielded them slightly. He could defend the position and they wouldn't be trapped if they were caught unawares.

He set the orange box down and brushed aside an area that would do for sleeping. "Did you take all the survival packs last night?" He'd slept rough before, but he wanted Morgan to at least have a blanket.

Of course, he'd also be willing to snuggle close for warmth. He was generous like that.

"No, there were several still left. Outer edge of the wreckage towards the south." She sank down onto a boulder and hefted the beacon up, staring at it as if she could uncover its secrets. "Bring me back any tools you find," she said absently.

That was his dismissal, then. Cipher made it quick, aware the enemy could still lurk and that Morgan was sitting alone with no weapon to protect her. *He* was her weapon, her protector. So he had to be quick.

Finding the packs took little time, and he grabbed two, just in case. Tools were another problem. The ship was the finest available, and allowed for a single pilot to handle her without issue. An auto-mech took care of the machinery and fixed problems before they bloomed into something terrible. He also took the ship in for routine maintenance, so he didn't *need* to keep a set of tools handy.

Still, he looked. There had to be *something*. The ship was made of metal, most of it now twisted and scorched on the ground. What were tools except for metal bits in fancy shapes?

He struck gold when he found pieces of the auto-mech strewn around a still steaming hunk of metal. He had to be careful, knowing he might be close to the remains of the engine. He was able to pry several instruments out of the body of the mech and hoped they would be enough to help Morgan. He needed to get back.

She looked up when he approached and the beacon looked no different.

He held out the handful of tools and her face brightened. "I could kiss you right now!" She set the beacon aside, jumped up, and swiped the tools from his hand.

Without meaning to, Cipher reached out and caught her wrist, holding her in place. "You could?" She'd been cold to him most of the day, a coldness he more than deserved. But he wanted to stoke the heat within her, to taste her and make her moan.

And if she was grateful for a few tools, he'd find even more to give to her, a whole hoard of tools she could curate to her heart's content.

Her eyes met his and she swallowed, throat working hard. There was heat in her eyes and a promise of temptation. All he had to do was lean in, pull her closer, and take.

The dragon deep within him burned. So did the man.

Her tongue darted out to lick her lips, and his cock twitched. This kind of need never came on so fiercely. But the entire world could fall away and it wouldn't matter so long as he had her.

She shook herself, as if recovering from a daze, and pulled her hand away.

Cipher let her go and didn't press the question.

"Thank you for the tools," she said quietly. "I'll get to work on the beacon."

Cipher would let her work. And figure out how to fix his mess.

CHAPTER
TEN

MORGAN HAD to get her mind back on the beacon and not on whatever weird feelings Cipher was conjuring up in her. Her wrist still burned from where he'd held her, imprints of his fingers etched into her memory. It hadn't been a tight grip, nowhere near hard enough to bruise.

And yet, for a moment, it had felt like he'd controlled her. If he'd pulled her just a bit, she would have come willingly. Eagerly.

She wanted him. And she hated herself a little bit for that. He'd made his feelings more than clear. At best, she was a means to an end. She'd get them off this planet and then they'd never see each other again.

Wasn't that what he was supposed to be to her? It was his beacon that he was working on, after all. With his tools. That he'd taken the time to scavenge for her.

Ugh!

She couldn't afford to go all soft. Bart's shitty offer was still ringing around in her head and she didn't know why she hadn't said a word about it to Cipher. If they were supposed to help each other, that seemed pretty important.

But had they ever made that agreement?

It made her thoughts stutter and she realized that, no, they really hadn't made any sort of agreement. Technically she didn't owe him anything.

That didn't mean she wanted to leave him stranded. She had to tell him about Bart.

She looked up to do so and was surprised to see that Cipher wasn't there. "What?" The word popped out, her old habit of speaking to herself always lurking.

She stood up from the boulder she'd chosen as a seat and winced at her stiff muscles. She must have been sitting for some time and zoned out. Had Cipher just taken off?

She couldn't see him in the debris field, but perhaps he was searching for more supplies. A glance against the wall of their little shelter showed open packs that had been dug through, useful items piled to the side.

No food.

She saw two water canteens, but none of the tell-tale meal bars or protein clay that was usually stored in survival packs.

So Cipher had likely gone to find food. Her stomach growled and she realized she hadn't eaten in quite some time. The light was getting long and darkness would fall soon.

Hopefully he was back before then.

She sat back down by the beacon and used the tools she had to get to work. They weren't the right tools, but she could fake it for now. She didn't know how long she'd been working, but she was squinting in the near darkness when she finally admitted defeat.

The beacon was fucked.

And so were she and Cipher.

She cradled her head in her hands and refused to let tears fall. This wasn't even the worst thing that had happened since she'd been dumped here. She'd almost died half a dozen times. This was just a broken piece of tech.

Maybe Cipher was important enough that someone would come looking, even without the beacon.

He hadn't said who he was, not beside his name and species. But she knew how rich guys talked. And he talked like the richest of them all. So maybe he was some super important CEO of a dragon corporation and his underlings were already in a fury looking for him. They'd be able to find his flight plan.

Maybe they'd be found.

Eventually.

His home planet could be anywhere. And if they were far away, it could be years, decades even, before someone thought to look on this dinky hunk of rock.

So what about Bart?

He couldn't be trusted. How stupid did he think she was, trying to entice her by paying what he already owed her and nothing more? But he needed her. His crew was full of mercs, not mechs. There might have been one or two people who could fix minor issues, but none who would dare fiddle with the engine and FTL drive itself. They all thought that one wrong twist of a knob would make the ship explode.

Nothing on a space ship was that fragile, but Morgan hadn't exactly clarified that for anyone. She'd wanted job security.

So much for that.

Or maybe that was exactly what this opportunity was. She could get off the planet, and get to safety. She'd probably have to sabotage the engine or something to make sure that Bart didn't throw her out the airlock the second whatever was keeping his crew in place was fixed.

But then he might imprison her and never let her leave.

It wasn't like he had anything against slavery.

Morgan groaned and slid all the way to the ground.

If Bart was acting in good faith, could she ask him to take Cipher on as a passenger? Cipher talked like he had money. Maybe Bart would accept a payment in exchange for safe travel. The ship didn't normally ferry people around, but that didn't mean they couldn't.

Of course, her old boss was just as likely to ransom him or sell him as give him safe passage.

Trusting Bart would be a terrible choice. But it was maybe her only option.

Maybe she wouldn't bring Cipher with her, but she could take his information and get a message out about his whereabouts the first time she hit a comm station. Then he'd just have to survive on the planet for long enough for his people to come find him.

She'd managed on her own for two weeks. He was a freaking dragon. He could survive indefinitely.

Talking it out with Cipher was the smart thing to do. And she wouldn't have been able to keep her thoughts in if he was actually there with her. But the more she thought about it, the more she worried that she shouldn't say anything.

Bart was the only way off the planet. What if Cipher told her not to go?

He wasn't the boss of her. She'd known him for a day. And she wasn't going to simply listen to him. But he could tie her up, or find some deep cave and keep her there until the idea was moot.

She'd never forgive him.

And why would he do that? It wasn't like he'd put her safety above his own rescue.

She was going to go freaking crazy if she thought about this anymore, and the dark wasn't helping. There was still just enough light to see by, but it wouldn't last for long. She shuffled over to the survival packs, but didn't find any firestarting kits.

Of course not. Why would a dragon need one?

She heard movement and froze. The shadows outside her little safe haven seemed to swirl, and she worried about that monster she and Cipher had fled the night before.

"It's me," said Cipher, stepping out of the deep shadows. He grunted and something hit the ground.

She heard him moving, and a moment later fire flared and she had to squint against the sudden brightness. She saw what he'd dumped on the ground. "Is that…"

"Monster meat. It's what's for dinner."

CHAPTER
ELEVEN

LEAVING Morgan alone had been a gamble, but Cipher was glad he'd taken it. He needed to keep her fed, and his own stomach was beginning to protest. That was the only way he could explain to himself why the monster meat smelled so damn good.

He'd butchered it as best he could and managed to cut strips for them that he threw on the fire. Hopefully the monster would taste better than the fish.

How could it smell so good? Like roses and sugar and something underneath that made him shift uncomfortably in his seat.

He'd never known the smell of meat could make his cock hard, but the monster was trying. Or maybe his mind was just fucked and he needed an outlet.

"Did you get anywhere with the beacon?" he

asked. He reached into the fire and flipped the meat, looking up when Morgan let out a shocked cry.

Her eyes were wide, one hand reaching towards him, the other covering her mouth. Then she blinked a few times and leaned in to get a closer look, though still far enough away to keep from letting her human limbs be scorched. "Dragon." It was an awed whisper.

He flipped the meat and pulled back, hand a bit warm from the flames. Right. Human. He flashed his unharmed fingers at her. "All good."

She shifted her seat until she was close enough that she could grab his hand and examine it. "Fire doesn't harm you?"

Her fingers traced over the line of his palm and Cipher had to hold back a groan. If she kept doing that, he would have to pull her close and let her feel all of him. Her hands might just drive him mad.

He craved her touch.

But he forced himself to answer. "It depends. Another dragon's flame could harm me. And if a fire burned hot enough and long enough, I might be injured. I don't think I would do well if I were submerged in lava. But a simple camp fire? Especially one I started? No, the fire does no more than tickle."

Her fingers stilled. "That sounds amazing. I wish I could do that."

And now would be the perfect moment to test his little theory. Test it, let her control his flame, and then take her until they were both spent. But he hesitated. It would take no effort at all to summon a small ball of his flame and hand it over to her. If she was his mate, she could manipulate it to her heart's content. If she wasn't, it would burn her.

He could quench the flame before it did more than singe her palms, but the idea of harming her made him ill.

He wouldn't be responsible for even a scratch. Not just to sate his curiosity.

Still, he summoned his own flame and let it sit in his palm for a moment before forming it into a ball and tossing it from hand to hand. Morgan's eyes followed raptly as he moved the flame, the fire making her nearly glow in the darkness.

He threw the ball of flame up and let it explode into thousands of sparks that rained down harmlessly and dissolved before they could reach them.

"Show off," she said, smiling.

He reached into the flame and pulled out the meat, which made her snort for some reason. They were using one of the canteens he'd taken from the survival packs as a plate. And since the meat had come off the animal in strips, it was easy enough to pile the canteen high, though he was careful with his balance. He didn't want to cover their dinner in dirt.

Morgan cautiously reached over and punched a strip between two fingers and examined it, holding it close and breathing in deep. "I must be hungry. I don't think food has ever smelled this good. Or made me…" Her cheeks reddened, and she quickly popped the food into her mouth before she could finish her sentence. "Oh shit," she said around a mouthful. "This is really freaking good."

Cipher confirmed that for himself by taking a strip and chewing carefully. Then another, and another, letting the flavor explode over his taste buds. Heat settled deep into his veins, and need flared even hotter. The more meat he ate, the worse it got, until his body was one throbbing pulse of arousal.

Morgan's own chest heaved, and she made a noise in the back of her throat that made him want to lay her down and take her right there. From the way a flush had taken her over, he didn't think she'd mind.

No. She wouldn't mind one tiny bit.

They'd eaten through all the food, and though his stomach was sated, his body was far from it. The need had taken him so quickly his mind reeled. He'd been sitting with his want of Morgan all day, the desire to take her, to make her his and keep her, a refrain in the back of his mind.

Not this insistence. Not this thing that was strong enough to almost drive him mad.

Morgan ran her hand down the front of her shirt, flicking open the top button of her pants. Her fingers teased the flesh still barely hidden by her oversized clothing.

And Cipher couldn't look away. His cock was an iron rod and if he didn't do something in the next minute, he feared he might explode.

"I think our dinner is having an effect on us," Morgan said with a surprisingly steady voice as she arched her hips up.

"Yes," was all he could manage. If he said more, he'd pounce on her. His control held on by a bare thread. It was a risk a person always ran when trying food from an alien planet. Usually, though, it led to a stomach, not a cock ache.

He had to be the gentleman. While his body was on fire with need, his mind was as clear as ever. The monster meat hadn't made him drunk. He edged away from Morgan, every scrape of his clothing against his skin a new and pleasurable torture.

"Where are you going?" she asked, hand snapping out and landing on his.

It rooted him in place and he froze. "Putting distance between us." Each word was its own struggle, but he was a lord and a warrior. He could do this. "Until the effect wears off."

The fingers of her other hand flicked at the next button on her pants. "Or you could stay."

Stars above and beyond, *yes*. He wanted her. She wanted him. They could lay together and sate one another until they were no longer under this strange spell.

And by then they would be too caught up in each other to care, bound together by something stronger than a strange reaction to food.

But still, he didn't want her regretting things once their bodies cooled. Once he had her, he intended to *have* her. And he was a dragon, he did not let go of things—or people—who belonged to him.

She had to be his mate.

He doubted he could have resisted so hard otherwise. But the thought that she might hate him in the morning was enough for him to think beyond his aching cock. "I don't want you to regret this." He was too focused on the sensations in his body to think of a lie, so the truth had to suffice.

Morgan pulled her shirt over her head, revealing full breasts that had been teasing him under her shirt all day. "Cipher? Get over here and fuck me."

CHAPTER
TWELVE

WHEN HER BODY wasn't drenched with need, Morgan might look back on this moment with a laugh. Aphrodisiac monster meat. Who would have thought?

But right now, she had a giant of a dragon looming over her, wicked heat in his eyes. Everything she wanted in one huge package. Her eyes flicked from head to toe and then back up again.

Yes. *Every* part of him was huge. Which might have been intimidating if she wasn't already wet enough to take a cock as big as her arm.

Her clothes rubbed against her skin and irritated her. And now that Cipher was on board for the ride, she pulled her pants off and stood naked before him. The flickering firelight probably hid more than it revealed, but his gaze was a caress.

And then his own clothes were gone in a flurry of movement and they were naked together.

Right.

Her skin was hot and ached to be touched, and at the same time she was so empty she could whimper. She'd been aroused before, was no stranger to lust. But this went beyond anything she'd ever felt.

An effect of their dinner? Or something about Cipher?

She feared it was the latter. But she didn't want to resist him, not one bit.

Cipher stepped forward and she breathed deep, taking in his masculine scent. Though mostly she smelled the crackling wood in the fire.

But the heat she felt came straight from his body, emanating out like he was a furnace.

Or a dragon.

His heat seeped into her, branding her. Standing so close was like being branded by a storm. Exciting. Electric. Deadly.

Need built inside her, making her jittery, and she couldn't let any more space come between them. She rubbed against him, wanting to ease the ache that had taken up residence low in her belly. The groan he let out as her skin met his only ratcheted up the heat.

This was nothing like she'd ever felt before. She knew the relief that could come from a night of fun.

But this desperation made her worry that a night with Cipher might ruin her for anyone else.

It was a risk she had to take. She couldn't walk away. And this had nothing to do with the monster induced arousal.

One of his hands cupped her breast and she arched into the touch. Her nipple beaded tight and she couldn't stop the filthy moan she let out. She would have begged for more, but he leaned in and captured her lips and swallowed down anything she might have said. His thumb brushed over the peak and pleasure shot through her, pooling in her core.

His hand trailed down her stomach, dipping lower until he found the wet heat between her thighs. A single finger traced the seam of her sex and she shuddered, arching into him. How could he have such an effect on her with just fingers and a kiss?

He could own her soul. If she wasn't careful, she might give it to him freely. And she needed to remember that he was a dragon. She couldn't become his hoard.

But her need drowned out her worries and everything else until all that existed was Cipher and the yearning for more of his touch.

Cipher's wicked lips smiled against her mouth and he pressed his thumb to her clitoris. A jolt of pleasure shot through Morgan and she gasped. His tongue took advantage of her open lips and delved in, tasting and teasing like he'd been born to do it.

He was touching her where she needed it most, his fingers sinking deep inside her, spreading her open and making her ready. A cry tore from her throat and she arched up into his touch. He added a second finger and curled them both, rubbing against that spot inside her that lit her up from the inside and made her beg.

Her hips moved of their own accord, needing more friction. She wanted him inside her. Now. An order flitted against her lips, but Cipher still kissed her and she couldn't take control of her tongue to speak. Not that it was any hardship to keep kissing him. He kept up the steady rhythm, drawing ever more pleasure from her body.

His own cock was iron hard and teasing between them, but somehow Cipher ignored it, determined to bring her to the heights of pleasure with only his fingers and a kiss.

She thought she would go mad with need. Her skin was too tight, her sex too empty. She would scream with the desire he'd fanned the flames of and beg for him to take her until she couldn't remember her own name.

If he thought she would simply let him take her like this, he was wrong. She was in this with him. And she wanted him just as desperate as she was. She wanted his control to snap and for him to back her against the wall and pound into her until she knew she would feel the imprint of him for days.

And to snap his control, she had to take it for herself. She pulled away from his kiss, even as her whole body protested. And while Cipher used those diabolical fingers of his, she used her own to reach out and wrap her hand around his stiff cock.

Cipher's breathing came fast and he clenched his jaw. Their eyes met and she saw a flame dancing in his. It was no reflection of the fire behind them. It was a firm reminder that she was taking a dragon to her bed. Well, her cave. And he was on the brink of losing his control.

She wanted him as wild as she felt, the utter abandon that this strange interlude allowed her. His eyes burned into her and she could see the battle he was waging. She smiled and writhed against him, watching as the flame in his eyes burned ever brighter and wild.

He let out a curse and grabbed her hips, and for just a moment she regretted that he no longer stroked between her thighs. But the regret disappeared when he yanked her against him so that she could feel every hard inch of his cock, the thick promise of pleasures to come. A cry of triumph escaped her and she tilted her head back, exposing her neck and not caring that he was an ancient predator that could finish her off right there. She felt no fear in his arms.

He took what she offered, nips and darts of his tongue a promise of all he could give her. He bit down on her earlobe, tugging just enough to make her whimper before letting go, and speaking gutturally against her. "You're mine."

It couldn't be true. This was one night out of time, an aberration in both of their lives that they might hold as a fond, or at least strange, memory. But the way he said it made her believe. Made her want to believe so hard that the ache in her heart overtook the ache in her body for a moment. She wanted to make the declaration right back to him, to stake some sort of claim that he couldn't deny.

But she choked the words back.

He wasn't hers.

She wasn't his.

This was one night out of time.

And she couldn't let herself forget it, no matter how good all of this felt. "Fuck me, Cipher. Show me."

He didn't need to be told twice. Cipher grabbed her hips and turned her around so that she was leaning over the edge of the boulder she'd used earlier to fix the beacon. Good. She needed it this way. If she watched him while he took her, she feared her heart might start getting ideas. But still, she couldn't resist a look over her shoulder. She spread her legs wide, giving him an open invitation to take her however he wanted. She only hoped he took her hard and fast, keeping this going until she was nothing but pleasure.

His hands on her hips were a hot brand as he pulled her back against him so that she could feel his thick cock teasing her entrance. She moaned in anticipation and writhed, wanting more.

And the same want must have been roaring through Cipher. There was no gentle lovemaking here, not once he was inside of her. He filled her up and she had to swallow past the feeling that he might be too much, too big.

He wasn't. He was fucking perfect.

And then he moved. And finally, Morgan could let go of all the fears and doubts that waited at the edges of her consciousness and just feel. He pounded into her, hard and fast from the start. It was exactly what she wanted, what she needed. But it wasn't enough even as it was almost too much.

She needed him. All of him. Whatever he would give her.

She angled her head back and looked up at him over her shoulder as he continued to drive into her. The flame in his eyes burned brighter than ever and she felt herself teetering on the edge of release. The sheer concentration on his face was almost a threat.

And a dark promise.

What would this man be like on another world? In another time?

What would he be like if he was truly hers?

It was her last thought as the pleasure swept her away, her body surrendering to his on a tidal wave. She yelled out his name, fingers grappling against the boulder she laid against, hoping for some sort of purchase as her body gave up.

Behind her, Cipher stiffened, finding his own release.

And as he came, he said her name.

It sounded almost like a prayer.

IT WAS dark out when Morgan opened her eyes and Cipher wasn't lying close. She saw him on the other side of the fire and it made her frown. And then the frown made her scowl. They'd fucked. Cuddles were not an obligation.

Though it might have been nice. The night around her was chilly.

That was a sure sign that the effects of the monster meat had worn off. While caught in the grip of its passion, she could have run naked through the tundra and not felt the cold.

Her body ached from all the ways that Cipher had taken her, and it certainly hadn't been just once. The effects of the meat had started to wear off after their second round, but neither of them had said a word.

And by the fourth round, her head was clear. And the only arousal she felt came straight from her desire for Cipher.

It had been a night out of time, one she would hold close and remember until she was an old lady, surrounded by cats. If she lived that long. Or got to a planet where cats existed.

Bart.

Shit.

In the sudden flurry of heat and need, she'd forgotten to tell Cipher about Bart. Or perhaps she'd never meant to. Her thoughts from before dinner were all muddled together. She knew the beacon didn't work and that they were stranded.

Unless she took Bart's offer and took her ride off on the hopes that a known scoundrel wouldn't betray her.

She had to try.

What would happen if she stayed here for any longer with Cipher?

Her emotions would get even more tangled up, that was for sure. And if he returned to the cold-hearted asshole who'd been with her before dinner, it would hurt. Of course, a bit of emotional pain would be nothing compared to what Bart could do to her if he was planning to betray her.

Again.

She could feel the edges of a headache coming on and forced herself to take several deep breaths to clear her head. She needed to be logical about this.

If Cipher weren't here, would she go with Bart?

Yes.

Would she still doubt Bart's intentions?

Yes.

But it would get her off this planet. If she was expecting a betrayal, she could plan for it. This wasn't like the first time. She wouldn't be new to the ship and so happy to have a job that she'd overlook the shady things the crew did.

Cipher grunted in his sleep and rolled to one hip, showing a wide swath of his naked back to her.

Morgan bit her lip and curled her hands into fists to keep from doing anything stupid, like scooting over and joining him. She'd never leave their shelter then.

But her body would be so satisfied that it would take her a long time to regret it.

She quietly and quickly found her boots and pulled them on. She'd put on the rest of her clothes before finally falling into her doze. The dragon on the other side of the fire might be able to sleep shirtless, but her human body had its limits.

Still, she hesitated before leaving. She had no way to leave a note. Would he worry when she was gone? Or feel betrayed?

Was this a betrayal?

There was only one sure path off this planet and she was taking it without giving him a chance to join her.

But if she gave him a chance, he might stop her. She didn't know if Bart would hang around waiting. He might not have had much choice, but eventually he might figure out how to allow his ship to limp to the nearest space station or settled planet.

And then she eyed the beacon. If only she could fix it. Unfortunately, something had fried the internal circuitry and without new parts, it was nothing but a bulky orange box.

She looked back at Cipher and made a vow to herself. The first chance she got, she'd look up where dragons came from and send them a message about where Cipher was. And if that didn't yield any results, she'd put enough credits together to hire a crew to come get him.

He wouldn't be stuck here forever.

She crept out of their shelter and into the dark night. The moon was fat and bright in the sky, giving her enough light to see by, and casting long shadows. But it was still dark enough that she had to step carefully. She didn't want to accidentally end up in the middle of the debris field and trip over something. There were no medbots here to heal a broken leg, and they'd left all the regen gel back at her camp.

She hadn't made it far when noise behind her made her freeze.

Another monster?

Slowly, she turned, and found Cipher there, eyes strangely illuminated in the night. He was breathing hard. "Where do you think you're going?"

CHAPTER
FOURTEEN

CIPHER RARELY WOKE ALONE when he went to a woman's bed. And if anyone left before sunrise, it was him. So hearing footsteps moving around their shelter and eventually getting fainter had confused him for a moment. He'd thought, perhaps, that Morgan had walked away to deal with her body's urgent demands.

Then she hadn't come back and worry set in.

And that worry turned much darker when he found her walking on the edge of the debris field, steadily getting farther from their shelter. She didn't look like a woman about to return to sleep.

She looked like a woman running away.

It wasn't safe.

And she was going the wrong way if she intended

to go back to camp. Was she turned around? Or was something else going on?

Morgan's shoulders slumped, and she looked anywhere but at him. "I thought you were asleep." She said it like a confession.

"Did you think I'd sleep deeply when we could be attacked at any moment?" Had she doubted he would keep her safe? He protected what was his.

"I didn't realize you could control how deeply you slept." She looked over her shoulder in the direction she'd been walking. Looking for someone? "I knew leaving was a bad idea, but it was the only choice. It's later than I thought."

"It's the middle of the night. This place is dangerous. Are you trying to head back to camp?" And then it occurred to him. "Is this… about what we did?" He'd worried she'd regret it, that she'd wake beside him and accuse him of taking advantage. Or that she'd call it a mistake.

When their passion had finally started to release them from its grip and she'd turned away to put her clothes back on, he'd taken that as the first sign of rejection. He'd wanted to pull her into his arms and sleep beside her, but he'd forced himself to stay on the other side of the fire and not push for more.

He'd planned to begin his seduction in the morning.

Morgan had to be his mate. No one else could make him feel the way he was feeling for her, certainly not so soon.

"No!" Morgan's eyes widened and she shook her head violently. "Not at all. That was… that was… it was fine."

Fine. Just the rating of performance a man wanted to hear.

She continued. "I should have told you this earlier. Bart found me in the wreckage while you were fighting the crew."

"What?" he could feel his flame flaring and tried to take control. The urge to shift and fly long and far beat at him. But he wouldn't walk away from this conversation. Not until he understood exactly what Morgan was saying.

"Something is wrong with his ship. There's no other mech on board. He offered to pay me what he owes me and dump me at the nearest space station if I get them up and running. I was going to send word to your home planet about you the second I got to a communication terminal." There was a note of pleading in her voice.

He forced himself to ignore it. "You don't know where I'm from."

"How many planets could have dragons?" she shot back, and he had to admit she was right. Vemion was the home of dragons, and they only had a few outposts in their chunk of the galaxy.

"And you couldn't have mentioned this before leaving?" It wasn't a solid plan. It was the bare scrap of an idea. But their situation wasn't far from desperate. This could be her only ride home. If it weren't for one problem. "Bart will betray you."

Morgan made a frustrated sound. "Do you think I haven't been trying to solve that problem all day? He might betray me. He might chain me up in the engine room and leave me there to fix things. Or he might actually keep his word. I've been figuring out a workaround. Sort of."

"Sabotage?"

"Okay, clearly the workaround isn't that clever," she muttered.

Despite himself, Cipher smiled. But his ire came right back. "You can't go."

"You can't stop me." She said it with confidence, but they both knew the truth.

He was a dragon. He could do anything.

He forced himself to stop arguing for a moment. He needed to *think,* and it was difficult with righteous fury flowing through his veins.

Morgan had a ride off the planet. It might be the *only* ride off the planet. Bart needed her alive to fix his engine, and he likely wasn't stupid enough to kill her right after she did. Something else could go wrong.

And a man likely to double cross his allies expected the same in return.

He wouldn't kill her. Not until he was sure he could find another mech. And that meant he'd need to land at a space station or on a planet. He *might* be able to kidnap a mech from another ship, but space was so huge that the likelihood of passing by close enough for piracy was nil.

She was right to leave. But he would help her as much as he could, even if he couldn't go with her. Bart had little reason to keep *him* alive. "When you land, *wherever* you land, don't wait for payment. Just run. If you find station security, bribe them."

Morgan scoffed. "With what credits?"

"Tell them Lord Cipher of Vemion guarantees it. Contact Vemion. I have two brothers, Storm and Drake. One of them will pay the bribe and fetch you. You can bring them to me. But you have to get your-self away from Bart." He hated the thought of leaving her alone, but she'd survived on Bart's ship before. And she'd proven her mettle by surviving two weeks of living rough.

She could do this.

"Did you say *lord?*" Disbelief suffused her words. "What?"

The sound of a blaster charging up caught his attention, and Cipher jerked his head beyond Morgan and saw a cluster of four people standing on a slight hill, weapons pointed straight at them.

"A lord?" Bart sounded as if he'd just found a pile of gold. "Dear Morgan, you're already proving your worth. Get them on the ship."

And before Cipher could make a move against them, someone fired at him and he fell to the ground.

CHAPTER
FIFTEEN

MORGAN GLARED at the cuffs on her hands. They weren't chained together. That would defeat the purpose of stashing her in the engine room. She could hear the persistent hum of the idling engine through the wall behind her.

She could work on the engine and access the nearest washroom. The cuffs prevented her from moving any further. There was a laser tether in the engine room and it pulled her back if she strained too hard against it.

She wished they'd used traditional chains. She could cut a chain.

Which, of course, was why they were relying on tech.

After Cipher went down, Bart and his crew wasted no time teleporting up to the ship. She had no idea where Cipher was, but wherever it was, she hoped he didn't hate her. Maybe that wasn't the worst possible outcome, but she was refusing to think of what else Bart could be doing to him.

He was a dragon lord. She kept that thought firmly in mind. Someone like that would catch a very high ransom. Bart wouldn't do too much damage.

A freaking dragon lord. A dragon lord she'd had *sex* with. A dragon lord who'd spent the last day and a half running hot and cold, all the while protecting her and making sure she was fed and bandaged.

She'd met petty lords before. Most of them were bandits who'd managed to carve out their own little chunk of space and controlled it with violence and graft. But those lords didn't speak like Cipher. And they certainly didn't allow brothers to live.

Family stole territory.

So he was probably the other kind of lord. The kind that came with stacks of money, big houses, and being on a first name basis with royalty. Her mind reeled at the thought. She was just a normal woman who'd spent most of her life on a space station until she'd signed on with a crew, desperate to see the universe.

Her ears buzzed and her teeth chattered as the engines spun up. Bart hadn't bothered to throw away her things, though they'd clearly scavenged through them and taken anything of value. Her communicator was long gone, and so was the cute necklace she'd bought after her first payday.

Assholes.

But she found her ear protectors after a short search through the pile of clothes that had apparently not been stylish enough to steal.

Spinning engines meant they were about to take off. Had Bart lied about the engine problems? Why?

They put on a burst of speed, and she immediately heard something was wrong, even though her ear muffs. The FTL drive screeched, even as the standard engine purred and ran like it was actually worth the credits Bart had refused to spend on it.

Without FTL, though, they were stranded. She didn't know the exact coordinates of this planet, but it was out of the way. And Bart often carried the kind of cargo that made sending out a distress call impossible. If the wrong people caught him hauling slave control chips, he'd be in deep trouble.

And if the *right* people, the kind who had no qualms about slavers, found him, they'd be as likely to steal the chips as to help him.

After running for a few minutes, the engine slowed again, idling back so that only the quality of life systems were running. Otherwise, they were adrift.

And probably out of teleport range of the planet.

Morgan could work on the FTL while the regular engine was running, but it was possible that Bart didn't know that. And she wasn't about to tell him. She'd heard the FTL whine like that before and already knew the fix. Two screws were loose and a lever needed to be jiggled. Then they'd be on their way.

She'd never show Bart how to do it. The second she did, she lost any leverage she had.

And she needed to figure out how to sabotage the ship in a way that forced him to land at a space station. Hopefully one that didn't allow slavery. If they landed and she managed to send out some sort of distress call, perhaps station security would board the ship and free her and Cipher.

Of course, station security across the galaxy always had a palm open for bribes. And Bart knew exactly which palms to grease.

It felt hopeless. And Cipher must hate her.

Did he think she'd conspired with Bart to get him on the ship? Bart would try and divide them. He'd try and make Cipher think that Morgan was happily working for the crew.

Cipher wouldn't believe it. He knew enough about her to know that wasn't true.

Right?

Had she convinced him before Bart found them?

Would a dragon lord believe a human?

She had to stop torturing herself. She couldn't know what Cipher thought until she found him. And then she had to free him. And they somehow had to overpower the crew and hijack the ship.

Escape pods were another option, but she didn't exactly relish landing right back where she'd started.

The door to the engine room clanged open, and Bart stood illuminated by the bright lights of the hall behind him. "Are you settling in?" he asked as if she were new crew and not a prisoner.

Morgan glared at him. She would have reached for a wrench to bash him over the head, but he could dart out of range in a step and then he'd send someone in to work her over. Escaping while covered in bruises would be even harder.

"Ah, well, we still plan to let you off, just like I said, but you've got to get us to Corsica Station first. Nav shows it's our nearest option." He looked beyond her to the panel that would expose parts of the engine. "You haven't gotten to work?"

What could she even say to that?

But the prospect of Corsica Station was a good one. It was large, relatively safe, and the guards that ran it were bought and paid for by the mercs who already lived there and didn't tend to take bribes from random ships.

If she could make it off the ship, she and Cipher just might have a shot.

Bart's face darkened, and he was suddenly made of threat. He hadn't moved any closer, but somehow he seemed to occupy the room. "I know you can fix this ship. I've seen you babysit the FTL a dozen times. We're jumping in fifteen minutes. If it doesn't work, I'm throwing you out the airlock and selling your friend to the deepest, darkest resource mine I can find. No one will come to rescue him. Do you understand?" He took two steps forward.

Morgan's tools were all out of reach, but she was only one step away from a control panel. She laid her palm flat on it. "Lay a finger on me and I'll overpower the engines. We'll explode."

Bart stopped. He held his hands up, expression clearing somewhat. "You have fifteen minutes."

She slumped back in relief when he left. It would take her less than a minute to temporarily fix the issue.

But should she?

CHAPTER
SIXTEEN

FOR EXACTLY SIXTEEN seconds after waking up, Cipher's head was full of fuzz. Then his metabolism chewed whatever was in his system up and spit it out. His head cleared and he stood, taking in his surroundings.

Standard ship cell. Heavy door, smooth walls, no cot or other designated place to sleep. It was basically an empty closet that was reinforced to keep whatever it stored in.

Cipher rammed the door anyway.

It didn't do anything except give him a sore shoulder.

Definitely reinforced.

He wasn't chained, and that was their mistake. They hadn't even put a laser tether on him, instead trusting that the cell would hold him in place. Fools. A human *might* have been trapped, but Cipher was no human.

The air around him seemed to ripple, and his ears popped as the ship jumped to FTL.

Cipher bared his teeth. It was good and bad news. He had his confirmation that Morgan was on the ship somewhere. But she was also doing Bart's bidding. What had he threatened her with?

It didn't matter. The man had signed his own death warrant when he captured them. Cipher wasn't letting him escape.

But first, he had to escape.

He looked at the door with new eyes. But the only way to even tell it was a door was because of the rivets and seam around it. There was no handle. He tried prying at the seam for several minutes, but that did nothing except hurt his fingers.

Cipher stepped back, taking deep breaths to steady himself. He looked around again, this time for sensors rather than an escape route.

How was Bart's fire suppression?

On his own ship, it was rated for dragons. Even in space, dragons sometimes summoned their flames, since it was as natural as breathing. But a human ship would have a lower tolerance.

On a ship that didn't carry prisoners, doors would automatically unlock and he'd have a *very* short opportunity to run to the nearest airlock before all the air in the cabin was vented.

A prisoner ship would likely vent their prisoners along with the air.

No open flame, he decided. Not yet. If he had to guess, Bart would release his prisoners on the assumption he could round them all up as soon as the fire was taken care of. He wouldn't want to lose his money. But Cipher wasn't sure enough to bet his life.

But fire wasn't the only way he could make heat.

It was harder, and painful, unlike a simple flame. Cipher summoned his fire to his left hand but didn't let it manifest. In his other skin, he could do this across his whole body until his scales glowed a fiery orange.

He only needed his hand for now.

He tried the door first, but it wasn't affected by the glowing heat of his hand. He could lean against it all day and it wouldn't melt.

The wall, however, was a different story.

As soon as his fingers touched it, the material began to sizzle. Sweat poured down Cipher's spine and he knew he had to do this fast. Once he was through the wall, anyone on the other side of it would know something was wrong. And it was possible that he was already setting off sensors like crazy.

He couldn't worry about that now.

It took forever. Or, at least, it felt that way. He

feared he'd burned his hand off, it was so hot, and he couldn't feel his fingers as he commanded them to curl into a fist and punch through the wall.

But once he made the first breach, the rest were easier. And before long, he had a hole *just* big enough for him to shimmy through.

He did, not bothering to wait until the bits of the wall he'd compromised cooled off. He was a dragon; a little heat didn't matter.

Outside his cell was an unguarded hallway. It had to be monitored by cameras, and someone would surely come for him soon. But now Cipher had room to maneuver.

And he had to find Morgan.

The engine would be in the heart of the ship, the place least exposed to space or any sort of enemy fire. Standing where he was, he didn't know which way would lead him there, and there were no helpful maps lining the walls.

Instead, Cipher listened. And he heard a faint rumbling.

The FTL engine.

It would be a roar in the engine room, and it would call him where he needed to go.

Or it should have.

He quickly found the reason there weren't any guards. The hallway was sealed as tightly as his cell.

It turned out Bart was not a stupid man.

But Cipher was right next to the airlock that was acting as a barrier between him and the rest of the ship. And now he was willing to gamble with his life.

He turned away from the airlock and let his fire go, not letting up until the walls were blackened and the ceiling had caught fire.

An alarm sounded and bright lights flashed. Cipher pressed the emergency exit button on the airlock, and it opened just long enough to let him inside. Then the door slid closed, and he watched through a thick, transparent panel as his fire disappeared as if nothing had happened.

The oxygen had been vented.

And they'd really know he was free now.

The ship jolted as it fell out of FTL in response to his fire. They couldn't continue on until they assessed the damage.

He had to get to Morgan.

Now Cipher ran.

He let his instincts guide him, and he was shocked that he didn't run into another soul. Bart had to be working with a skeleton crew. Or, perhaps, the ship was more damaged than he thought and they were simply doing their best to limp to safety.

The roar of the engine—the standard one, not FTL —got louder, and Cipher finally rounded a corner to see a door standing open.

He heard a feminine yell.

Bart was dead. Perhaps he was still standing, but the second Cipher got his hands on him, the slaver would pay.

The scene in the engine room was something he'd be seeing in his nightmares for the rest of his life. Bart loomed over Morgan and had his hands wrapped around her throat. Morgan's arm flailed out as she reached for a wrench she couldn't quite wrap her fingers around.

And her struggles were getting weaker by the second.

With a roar, Cipher threw himself at Bart. The wise move would be to snap the man's neck and call it done.

But Cipher wanted to make him pay. There would be nothing fast here.

CHAPTER
SEVENTEEN

BLACK DOTS DANCED in the corner of Morgan's vision, and no matter how hard she tried, she couldn't suck down a breath around the steel grip Bart had on her neck. She tried to struggle, tried to reach for the wrench she *knew* was right *there*.

But her arm was too short. Or the table was too long.

She brought her knee up, trying to land a blow to a sensitive area, but the angle was all wrong and she barely swiped against his thigh. He didn't even seem to notice.

Fear warred with anger, and they both warred with oxygen deprivation. Was this really how it all ended?

And then, suddenly, Bart's hands weren't on her anymore and her throat burned with the sudden ecstasy of air.

Cipher!

He was like an avenging demon, smoke coming off him in an endless stream as he threw Bart against the wall beside her and pummeled his stomach with punishing blows.

"Be careful!" she tried to warn, but it came out scratchy and barely audible. Her throat needed time to recover. Still, they were in the engine room and there were enough things that could go wrong. She didn't want to survive Bart only to have Cipher accidentally make the engine overheat.

Cipher took Bart to the ground and pinned him there, his face a mask of fury. He'd shifted to that other form of his, where he had claws and the first hint of fangs, half man, half monster.

And he'd come for her.

Maybe she should have been afraid at how easy he showed this beastly side, but all Morgan could feel was relief.

He'd come. And they were *going* to get out of this.

Before Cipher could land another blow, the emergency tone sounded and a feminine voice came over the intercom. It might have been Skull, but Morgan wasn't sure. She was terrible at identifying voices over the crackling system.

"We've dropped into Dominion territory, captain. Almost on top of one of their warships. We're being hailed. We have three minutes to respond before they fire on us. I need you up here." The system cut out.

And Bart gave a gurgling laugh as he watched Cipher freeze. "What are you going to do, lordling? You've landed us in dangerous territory."

Something froze in Morgan's chest, and not even Cipher's fire could heat it up. The Dominion was a growing power in this region of space, having swallowed up its home solar system and moved on to the next dozen habitable planets over the course of a century.

They executed anyone suspected of being a slaver and threw anyone officially suspected of any other crime into their resource mines for a minimum of a year before sending them on to trial.

And they shot trespassers out of the sky.

There were jobs to be had in the Dominion, but crews were cautious about entering. And if Bart said the wrong thing, they'd all be dead.

But Cipher wasn't ready to let him go. His hand tightened on Bart's collar, as if he was going to hold him up to punch him some more. Then he relented and let the man drop.

"You're putting Morgan and I on that warship," Cipher informed him. "Tell them you rescued us from a wrecked ship and we're looking for passage to the nearest Dominion space station."

Bart actually laughed at that, and the blood

between his teeth made it a gruesome sight. "You'll tell them to blow me out of the sky the second you're clear."

Cipher made a sound of frustration, and it must have been his plan. He grit his teeth, jaw clenched hard enough she could see the muscles tic. "You have my word we will say nothing to the ship. We will head straight for the station. You can go on your way."

If her throat had been working properly, Morgan would have protested. Bart needed to pay for what he'd done to them, he couldn't just get away with it.

But Cipher had rightly guessed that this might be their only way out. And time was running short.

"Very well," Bart relented.

The intercom crackled again. "Captain, really need a response. One minute."

Bart turned to her. "Patch me through to the bridge."

She glared at him. "Undo the tether first." The words were barely audible, but she held up her hands so he could be certain of what she meant.

"No time," he insisted.

She just wriggled her fingers.

With a curse, he reached into his jacket and pulled out a small remote device. He hit two buttons and the cuffs around her wrists disengaged and fell off.

Plenty of time.

She reached behind her and engaged the intercom

on their side. She gestured for Bart to speak. He glared at both of them. "Let them know we've run into a slight repair emergency and temporarily dropped out of FTL."

Cipher cleared his throat.

Bart shot a rude gesture his way before carrying on. "And tell them we have two passengers who are requesting safe passage to the nearest Dominion station."

"Sir?" Skull asked.

"Do it," Bart commanded.

A moment later, Skull's voice surrounded them. "Confirmed, sir. We've been given leave to take an hour to repair. We must report back to request more time if we need it. And they're sending a shuttle. It will be here in ten minutes."

The curses that streamed out of Bart's mouth were creative even by ship standards, and no one knew how to curse more than a crew. He glared at both of them. "Have you stranded us in dangerous territory, you ungrateful excuse for a mech?"

With Cipher standing right there and the promise of freedom flying their way, Morgan had nothing to fear. "The ship should fly. You'll make it to your next station. Upgrade your machine if you want to go farther."

He looked ready to lunge at her, but Cipher leaned forward just enough to remind Bart of his presence, and Bart froze. "You're more trouble than you're worth," he spat at Cipher. "Now come on. I'll take you to the dock. You're not wandering my ship alone."

Bart made Morgan lead, with Cipher right behind her. No wonder he didn't trust the dragon at his back, but she was perfectly comfortable with it. It was only once they were waiting beside the airlock where the shuttle would dock that she started to realize what was about to happen.

They were freely flying into Dominion space.

That could be bad.

Morgan hadn't been a mech on many ships, but all independent ships tended to do a little… off the books freelancing from time to time. And not all of it legal. She didn't *think* there would be any warrants out for her in the Dominion, but of all the places to get arrested across the galaxy, the Dominion was low on the list.

Staying trapped on Bart's ship would be even worse.

Bart had retreated far enough away so he was out of reach if Cipher got violent, which gave them something approaching privacy.

Cipher reached out and grabbed her hand, giving it a squeeze. "All will be well. We're safe now."

She looked up at him and her breath caught. He was looking at her with the kind of intensity usually saved for the bedroom. Or a conveniently placed shelter in the rocks, if aphrodisiac meat had anything to do with it.

She wanted to go up on her toes and kiss him. Wanted to ask him if, perhaps, they could take some time for themselves without anything influencing them.

And she almost did it. But then the proximity alarm sounded as the shuttle arrived.

Safe. They were going to be safe.

So why did it feel like they were about to walk into the lion's den?

CHAPTER
EIGHTEEN

THEIR SHUTTLE PILOT was a polite enough Dominion officer who informed them that the entire shuttle was full of crew ready to take their leave at the nearest space station, which happened to be right on the edge of Dominion territory and free space.

Cipher was quickly swallowed up with a group of officers who talked and joked with him like he was one of them, while she ended up sitting near the pilot and watching the nav screen through the entire ride.

She knew what station they were going to. Corsica. Exactly where Bart had been headed. It wasn't exactly accurate to call it a Dominion station. Sure, it paid taxes to the king, but it was a territory unto itself.

But that was fine. Frankly, she was happy they were on the edge of the territory. It would make finding jobs that took her far away from this sector easier to find.

Where was Cipher going?

She looked down the narrow hallway to where he was laughing with the other soldiers. As if he could sense her gaze, his head snapped up and their eyes met. He gave her a soft smile and she couldn't help but return the expression. Then another soldier caught his attention and he looked away.

So much for that.

It didn't matter. Maybe this was her sign to go home. She'd had plenty of space adventures to last a lifetime. One kidnapping was more than enough. And she didn't want to get snarled in the dark world of people-trading ever again.

But there was nothing for her back home. She was out in the black to make a life for herself. Returning home would be the ultimate failure.

She had to find a way to make a new home for herself.

"So what was that all about?" the pilot, a woman named Neemi, asked. She wore her bright red Dominion uniform with pride. Her purple hair was pulled back into a tight braid, but strands of it seemed to sparkle in the dim light of the cabin. Her skin was similar in tone to Morgan's own, though a little darker and with a more orange undertone. But she might have been confused for human rather than Domi if she were back on Earth.

"What was what?" Morgan didn't even know where to begin with what was happening between her and Cipher. They'd known each other for two very stressful days. And there was no way she was explaining the whole monster meat thing to a perfect stranger.

"Ships don't tend to fall out of FTL in our territory. And passengers certainly don't ask for passage. So what made you and your friend brave the terrifying Dominion?" She said the last with an exaggerated emphasis, as if she found the idea of her kingdom being feared hilarious.

Cipher was the one who'd promised not to say who Bart really was. He might have promised for both of them, but he hadn't gotten her permission first.

Still, Morgan was going to keep his word. She hated Bart. She hoped some patrol caught him with his ship full of illegal parts and threw him in the deepest, dankest prison they could find.

But the Dominion wouldn't arrest him. They'd blow his ship out of the sky. And she didn't want to be responsible for the deaths of everyone on board. Even if they were terrible people.

"It's as he said. Cipher and I were rescued from a crashed ship. However, our rescuers were not as nice about it as they could have been." She could still feel the imprint of Bart's fingers around her throat, though it must not have bruised, otherwise someone would have mentioned it.

Neemi's hand casually hovered over the comm button on her nav panel. "Did they try to enslave you?"

"No." And technically Morgan wasn't lying. Yes, she'd been tethered to the engine room, but Bart *had* promised payment. She hadn't given him the opportunity to renege on his offer.

Neemi pulled her hand away. "That's good. We've had slavers testing the edge of our territory lately. They must be dealt with swiftly."

Morgan was thankful for the weak light of the cabin as her cheeks flamed. She hadn't knowingly participated in Bart's crimes, but the Dominion wouldn't care. She slumped back in her chair and kept her mouth shut. Better that than accidentally saying something that might make Neemi turn against her.

It was more than an hour before they were hailed by Corsica Station, and another hour after until they could dock. Cipher was exchanging handshakes and back slaps with the officers while Morgan said a more tempered farewell to Neemi. This would be one of her more memorable shuttle rides.

Not many people could say they'd ridden with the Dominion and survived to tell the tale.

Morgan's mind reeled as she tried to think out her

next move. Exhaustion weighed heavy on her, and she hoped she had enough credits in her account to rent a private room. The station might have a free public room for sleeping, but free rooms were often crowded, hot, and smelly. She'd rather spend the credits.

If she had the option.

Then she needed to find a job. Every ship needed a mech, and Corsica Station buzzed with activity. She'd be able to hire on to a crew in a matter of days. Hell, she could head on down to the hiring desk and be on a ship in a matter of hours.

A yawn nearly broke her jaw. Yeah, sleep first. She needed to make sure she didn't end up on another crew like Bart's. She needed her brain firing on all cylinders for that.

Cipher was saying his final goodbyes to the rest of the crew straggling off the shuttle. She would have never guessed he was so good at making friends considering how they had started out.

Maybe that said something about her.

What would he do if she walked up to him and invited him to get a private room with her? She could imagine the fire in his eyes as he scooped her up and carried her to this fantasy suite. She remembered the feel of him inside of her, the delicious stretch and glide of his body moving with hers.

And then the dream dissolved as she remembered just how few credits she had. No dragon lord would want to stay in the level of room she could afford. And she wasn't about to invite him to pay for the room. She wasn't that presumptuous.

She couldn't do it anyway. Walking away already felt harder than it should have. They had a bond formed through adversity and it made everything feel *more*. He should have barely been an acquaintance. Instead, it felt like she was walking away from her oldest friend.

Or something more.

And what would it feel like if she did invite him back into her bed and he said no? What if these feelings were all one sided? He was a dragon *lord*. He could have anyone he wanted. There were probably dozens of fancy ladies and lords who'd do anything to have him, even for one night.

Morgan couldn't compete with that.

And she wasn't going to try. That way guaranteed heartbreak.

The smartest play was to walk away and hold the good parts of their days together close to her heart. The rest she could let fade into her memories. And eventually none of it would hurt.

But she had to be strong enough to walk away. And that meant she had to do all the talking.

Cipher stood at the edge of the walkway that led from the shuttle's dock to the main part of Corsica. He started to smile when he saw her, but something on her face must have given away what she intended to say.

"Thanks for the save," she said, injecting as much brightness into her tone as she could muster. "And I'm sorry you couldn't do more to Bart. Whatever you were planning, he deserved it. So if you ever cross paths with him again, punch him for me." She had to keep talking, had to make sure he couldn't get a word in. "You should be able to contact your brothers now. You'll be home in no time. And it shouldn't be hard for me to find a new crew. Anyway…" She backed up a step and stopped.

Oh, what the hell. This was her last shot. Better to live with a bit of heartache than regret.

Morgan stood forward, went on her tiptoes, and captured Cipher's mouth with her own. His hands clutched her hips, pulling her close. She poured her heart and soul into the kiss. Every dream she might have had, every future that couldn't be. She wanted the memory of Cipher's lips imprinted on her forever. When she was an old lady, she wanted to remember every second of this moment.

But before it could become anything more, she forced herself to let go and pull away. Flames danced in Cipher's eyes, and it was almost enough to make her throw caution to the wind.

Almost.

But she wasn't a complete fool. Not yet.

"Goodbye, Lord Cipher." She turned and hurried away before he could try to stop her.

If he tried to call after her, his voice was swallowed up in the sounds of the station all around them.

The kiss had her heart beating fast, and a new wave of energy washed over Morgan. When she reached a branch in the corridor, one way heading towards room rentals, the other heading deeper into the docks where she'd find the hiring desk, she headed towards the docks.

Getting off this station as fast as she could was her new priority. She feared if she stopped moving even for a minute, she'd turn around and seek Cipher out.

A ship mech and a dragon lord didn't belong together. Not for the long haul. And she wasn't going to run headlong into heartbreak. She'd had her taste of him, and that was more than most people ever got. She'd have to savor that one taste forever.

And another reason occurred to her as she weaved her way through the teeming crowd.

Bart had plenty of friends. And he was on his way to Corsica. He could sour the job market here for her with just a few whispers. And he could do it across this half of the galaxy.

But if she was already on a ship by the time his message got out, if she had already proved herself... maybe it wouldn't be such a big deal. She wanted to stand on some principle that she wouldn't take work from someone who considered Bart a trustworthy source, but she couldn't. The man had been working these stations for two and a half decades. And he kept his shadier dealings well hidden. To many, he was simply a successful merc with a crew who often survived their jobs. That made him a good captain in many eyes.

And he had enough friends who *did* know about his shadier dealings that Morgan didn't dare start spreading rumors. She'd end up dead and in the station's incinerator in a blink.

When she made it towards the hiring wing, she started asking around before heading straight for the job board. Half of hires came from word of mouth, and she wasn't completely friendless. But she didn't know any of the crews looking for a mech.

And none of the crews seemed to want *her*.

She didn't have references handy, which was a bit of a problem. She could easily prove herself with a simple test or two, but no one was willing to take that chance. And as she moved from one captain to another, she began to wonder if Bart had spread the word ahead of his arrival.

Or if he was already on the station.

She wanted to say it was impossible, but his FTL drive had been fully functioning when she left him, and the shuttle she and Cipher had taken hadn't used

FTL. The ride that had taken them hours could have happened in a blink for Bart.

"Morgan?" The grizzled voice cut through the crowd, and Morgan smiled as Hort hobbled her way.

He'd been on Bart's crew when she hired on, but had quickly left, finding fault with the way Bart ran his ship. He'd said it was time to retire. The man had to be nearing seventy, and age marred his old merc's face. He'd been a captain himself once, but now just wanted to ride around the galaxy and see the sights.

She wouldn't have expected to see him here. A man with a history as long as his had to expect trouble at the edge of the Dominion. Then again, maybe that was why Hort was here.

"Hort!" She clasped his hand and then yelped as he pulled her into a tight hug. "It's good to see you."

"You too, girlie. You're a sight for sore eyes." He pulled away from her and his eyes snagged on her neck.

Morgan swallowed hard, and the movement scratched against her throat. Had bruises bloomed during the shuttle ride? She hoped not. She didn't need awkward questions. "How have you been? I didn't expect to see you in the Dominion."

A loud laugh boomed out of his chest, but no one looked their way. "I was in the area. And I've got a job, if you're looking for work."

"Yes! Absolutely!" She accepted before she could

even begin to doubt. She needed work. "I can leave as soon as you're ready. Can I bunk on the ship?"

Hort put a hand on her shoulder and squeezed just a little too tight. "Yeah, come this way."

The first hint of alarm flared at the edge of her mind. There was something off in Hort's voice. And when she tried to stop walking, he tugged on her arm. He was an old man, and Morgan didn't want to hurt him by resisting, so she changed tactics. "What's the job?"

"I need a mech. Does the rest of it matter?" He led her past where the other captains were hiring, and the halls quickly dimmed and the people all but disappeared.

"Kind of, yeah. Do you have a ship? I thought you retired." He was walking so fast she had to trot to keep up.

"Here, take her." Hort shoved her beyond a heavy door and pressed a button on the wall. The door started to slide closed.

Leaving Morgan alone with Bart.

CIPHER'S MIND still reeled from watching Morgan walk away.

Did she really think that was *it?*

At the very least he deserved a chance to talk to her, to say his own farewell. And once he started speaking, he'd make sure she understood that there wouldn't be a farewell. Not if he could help it.

He still hadn't seen beyond a doubt that she could control his flame. Nor had he shifted into his dragon form so that she could try to communicate telepathically with him. But he *knew.*

It was just as the matchmaker said. He'd needed to take a journey. And he'd found her.

He wasn't going to lose her so quickly.

But as he stormed into the station, he forced his raging mind to calm down. If he approached her like this, she'd surely run. And he couldn't blame her. Who wouldn't run from an angry dragon?

Perhaps the smart move would be to take a room for the night, find a ship he could hire to take him home, contact his brothers, and give both of them a few hours to come to terms with everything that had happened in the last two days.

Cipher was done playing smart.

If he waited, his mate might get away.

He'd had a plan, one he'd been concocting during the entire shuttle ride while he spoke with the Dominion officers. He'd find the nicest suite available, invite Morgan to join him, and woo her like the dragon lord he was. Half the conversation had been dedicated to figuring out where would be the best places on the station to take her.

The other half had been subtly ensuring they wouldn't think that Morgan had anything to do with Bart or any other slaver's crew. The Dominion didn't allow ignorance as a defense for crimes committed.

But he'd get her away from here soon enough.

When he found her.

She had to be just as exhausted as he was. They'd been up for more than a day at this point, certainly. He wasn't going to count a bout of mercenary induced unconsciousness as a nap. So she'd find a room.

That gave Cipher his direction. He headed towards the cheapest sector of the station, knowing that

Morgan must be short on credits. There was also a section where visitors could sleep for free, but he thought she might try and avoid that.

But when there was no record of her room rental, something he'd determined by parting with credits of his own, he went back and checked the free quarters.

She wasn't there either.

Could she have purchased a more expensive room? The difference in price was negligible for him, but it would have represented a significant amount of credits for Morgan. And she was a practical woman. If there were cheap rooms to be had, she would have taken one.

He checked the cheaper mess halls and didn't find her. But if she was hungry, there were vending machines lining the halls, so she might have fed herself some other way.

Had she tried to hire onto a crew? Was she leaving so soon?

With no other ideas, Cipher headed down to the area where crews looked for new hires. It was teeming with people, many of who tried to flag him down and hire him before anyone else could.

An old human man gave him an assessing look before turning away.

No sign of Morgan.

Now worry started to flood in. He'd been holding

it at bay while he exhausted his search, but it was as if she'd simply vanished.

Was Bart on the station?

It was a possibility he didn't want to consider. But this station was closest to where they'd stalled in the Dominion. And if Bart used FTL, he would have beat them here by some time.

And he was certainly a man to hold a grudge.

He was about to turn around to go find a way to check the docking manifests when a commotion started up at the far end of the hiring section. A few mercs yelled, but a dark-haired woman barreled through them.

Morgan.

She looked up and their eyes met. Hers widened, but she ran straight towards him just as he heard a masculine voice scream behind her.

"A hundred credits to whoever catches that woman."

A few of the mercs moved in to intercept, but most of them stayed back. A hundred credits wouldn't go far on Corsica Station.

Morgan got close enough that Cipher could get between her and the mercs who were coming her way and Bart. He summoned his flame to his palm and let it dance. The mercs immediately backed off, the job no longer easy money.

Bart kept coming.

Cipher was tempted to throw the flame, but they were in a crowd of people and on a space station. Uncontrolled flame would be catastrophic.

Instead, he vanished the flame and ran behind Morgan, shielding her from any blaster shots that might come their way.

Something clattered behind them, but he didn't waste time looking back. "There has to be a checkpoint nearby," he said, trying not to pant. But talking and running weren't easy. "We just need to lead him to station security."

"I think he's already paid them off. There should have been half a dozen guards down there." Morgan was panting, and beginning to lose speed.

She couldn't run for much longer, and Cipher wasn't sure how long he could carry her at a run. If he'd been freshly rested, he could go for hours.

They reached a turn in the hallway and Cipher saw they had nowhere else to go. The hallway ended in an airlock, and beyond it through two thick, transparent doors was the startling blackness of space, only interrupted by the ships that hovered around the station.

Wherever they were, this had to be a restricted section. Guards were meant to be stationed by every airlock to prevent unauthorized entry or exit.

Cipher couldn't worry about that now.

He summoned his flame again and watched the

hallway, ready to strike. "Stay behind me," he warned Morgan.

"You—" Whatever she was going to say was interrupted by Bart turning the corner.

He had a blaster in one hand, but wasn't pointing it at either of them yet. "I just want to talk, Morgan dear."

Morgan was close enough behind him that he could feel her stiffen. "Why Hort? He hates you."

Bart barked out a laugh. "Is that what you think? Oh, little girl, you know nothing. He thought I should be doing live runs, not just supplies. That's why he left. Not enough money in it."

Live runs? Slaves, Cipher realized. Whoever Hort was, he'd wanted Bart ferrying ships full of captured people, rather than just the supplies to enslave them.

Morgan made a sound of distress, but she didn't come out from behind him.

This had to end. And though Cipher wanted Bart's blood, he'd do this without bloodshed if he could. If only to keep Morgan safe.

"Put the blaster down and walk away," Cipher said. He let his flame spark a bit. "We can let this go."

"Not a chance." With surprising swiftness, Bart shot the blaster.

Cipher dove away and took Morgan with him. But he couldn't stay in front of her and fight Bart.

"I'll be fine." Morgan pushed him towards Bart. "I know how to hide."

That was all the encouragement he needed. His flame was gone, vanished as they dodged the blaster shot. Cipher was tempted to summon it back. But the same instinct that kept him from throwing it before ruled him now. He wouldn't risk damage to the station, especially not when they were near an outer wall.

One unlucky shot could lead to catastrophic failure.

Cipher took a blaster shot to his side, but breathed through it and tackled Bart to the ground. Apparently the blaster wasn't at its most lethal setting.

Good to know.

Bart was fighting for his life and he knew it. Cipher managed to land a few blows, but the merc wriggled away and hit back just as well as Cipher gave. And Bart wasn't afraid to play dirty, aiming below the belt and for Cipher's back.

Cipher hit back just as hard. The fight went on and on until everything dropped away. He tasted his own blood in his mouth from one of Bart's luckier hits. But the mercenary was taking the harder beating.

His blaster had fallen away sometime in the fight and Cipher hoped Morgan had managed to snatch it. But if he looked away from Bart to check, this whole fight would be over.

It would be over soon no matter what. Dark circles danced in Cipher's vision and Bart's face was swelling up. One of them would drop soon, and Cipher needed to be the last one standing.

"Cipher, kick him away!" Morgan's command cut through the haze in his mind and he did what she said.

It was only as Bart went flying that he realized where he was and what she'd done. The inner airlock door slammed closed with Bart trapped in it. He scrambled for the button inside that would open the door, but Morgan kept her hand on the button on her side of the door which prevented him from opening it.

He glared at them and beat against the glass, but they couldn't hear.

Cipher stumbled over to her. He wanted to gather her up in his arms and never let go. But he doubted she would appreciate the blood that covered him. And she needed to keep her hand on that button until the station guards came.

She looked up at him with hope in her eyes. "You found me." If a glance could be a caress, she was touching him now.

"Always," he promised.

But before they could say any more, station guards surrounded them, blasters drawn and commands loud.

"I've put in a manual override on the airlock,

commander," one of the guards who carried a computer tablet rather than a blaster said.

The commander stood behind his men. "Good. Sir, ma'am, step away from the door and keep your hands in front of you. Now."

He and Morgan did as instructed. Two of the guards approached the airlock and Bart, who hadn't stopped screaming. The guards' blasters lit up red, indicating they were armed for a fatal shot.

They killed slavers on sight in the Dominion. And Bart knew that.

He shuffled back the two steps of space he had as the guards got closer. Then, before they could open their side of the door, he pressed the button that opened the door to open space.

For a moment, nothing happened, and Cipher thought it was another useless attempt.

Then an alarm blared and the outer door opened, sucking Bart out into the black.

IT DIDN'T HURT to have a dragon lord with you when questioned by guards, Morgan realized as she woke up in a very soft, very comfortable bed in the nicest suite on Corsica Station.

There were two whole bedrooms in the suite, something mind-boggling to consider compared to the tiny capsule room she would have rented. Her room would have consisted of a bed barely wide enough for one person, an entertainment screen, and a communal bathroom. There wouldn't have even been enough room to sit up.

She didn't want to imagine how many credits Cipher had wasted on this room. Thousands, at least.

But the rest was worth it. After two weeks on that terrible planet and two days of non-stop action, she needed the bed more than she'd ever needed one before. She glanced around for a clock, curious how long she'd been out. But there wasn't one on the wall.

What did it matter? She didn't have a place to be.

She threw the covers off and stretched, reveling in the warm temperature of the room and her nudity. She'd used the last of her strength the night before to stumble into the shower and wash off two weeks' worth of grime. Then she'd stumbled into bed, hoping Cipher might follow.

Instead, she'd slept alone.

Right.

Maybe she was reading too much into the big rescue. Maybe Cipher rescued every woman that crossed his path.

Maybe they needed to have an actual conversation.

Morgan groaned and collapsed back onto the bed. For a conversation, she needed clothes. Cipher might have seen it all before, but that didn't mean she was about to parade around naked.

So she needed to actually find her clothes. Were they in the bathroom?

After the fight with Bart, everything was a blur. Cipher had gone all lordly on the guards who'd wanted to take them in for questioning and then swept her away to the room. He'd promised her all would be taken care of.

Then he'd disappeared. Or, at least, she didn't remember seeing him after that.

She didn't relish putting her filthy clothes back on, but it had to be done. And she could buy something new later. Corsica had plenty of shops.

She pulled a blanket off the bed and wrapped it around herself so she could go in search of her old clothes. But when she opened the door to her room, she found a package waiting for her. When she picked it up, it squished in her hand like it was full of fabric.

She retreated back inside, closed the door, and opened the package.

It was a simple yellow dress with a purple collar and purple rings around the short sleeves. There was no underwear or bra with it, but when she pulled it on, she discovered it had a built-in bra, and it fell just below her knees, making the prospect of flashing someone unlikely. She still felt a little naked as she walked around her room, but it was better than walking around huddled in a sheet.

Had Cipher bought this for her? Or maybe fancy suites automatically came with clothes.

One way to find out.

She was suddenly nervous. After a full night's sleep, her mind was sharp. She was no longer riding the edge of panic like she had the night before. And, she realized, she might not have been acting completely rationally when she ran to find a job, trying to get off the station before she risked having a conversation with Cipher.

That was a shitty move. At the very least, he deserved to say his bit. If he had a bit to say.

She squared her shoulders and headed into the central part of the suite where a small dining table, food processing machine, and entertainment area were clumped together. The suite was spacious by station standards, but square footage still came at a premium.

Cipher was sitting plates on the table along with glasses of juice. He smiled at her when she entered. "Good afternoon."

"Afternoon?" Again, she saw no clock.

"You slept for fifteen hours." He patted one of the chairs, indicating it was for her.

Well, *that* would explain why she felt so rested. She looked over the spread and her mouth watered. She realized the last thing she'd eaten was the sex-meat and her cheeks heated.

Cipher must have read her mind or something. "I checked it all. We're fine."

Good enough for her. If Cipher wanted to talk, he'd have to wait. She dug in with gusto, eating all of the fruit and cheese on her plate before moving on to the toast and finishing it off with some kind of pastry that had just a hint of chocolate and cinnamon.

A feast. She couldn't remember the last time she'd eaten chocolate.

Her stomach sated, she drank the juice more slowly. It might have been orange juice in another life, but it had a strange, almost bitter undertone that gave it more depth. Whatever it was, it was good.

Cipher ate more slowly, and she took the opportunity to watch him. Was this how lords ate? Every bite so tiny and deliberate? She would expect a dragon to devour.

But maybe that was why he did it. A sign of his control.

She knew what it felt like when his control snapped. And she wanted to feel it again.

He finished the food and she cleared the table, putting their scraps and plates into the slot on the other side of the food processor. Everything got broken down, recycled, or burned on the ship.

When she turned, Cipher was right behind her, canvas sack in hand. "I took the liberty of purchasing a few more things for you. I'm sorry you had to leave all your belongings behind."

"On the planet? There wasn't much. But thank you." She knew how strained her credit account was and she wouldn't turn down free clothes. "You lost more than I did. Your whole ship."

He shook his head. "Not at all. I wasn't carrying much."

And there was more of the difference between them. If she crashed a ship she owned, she wouldn't rest until she'd put it back together piece by piece. She couldn't afford otherwise.

Morgan clutched the bag to her chest and side-stepped around Cipher. "Let me put these away."

She headed for her room, but he was right behind her. "Will you tell me what you think of the pieces?"

"Sure." She needed to put space in between them before she did something crazy, like jump him, wrap her legs around his hips, and hope he got the right idea. She opened the small wardrobe and set the canvas on a shelf. Then she reached in and pulled out the first thing she found.

Another dress.

But not like what she wore now.

There was nothing casual about the slinky fabric in her hands. It was black as the space around them, but as she shifted the fabric in her hands, it shimmered like there were stars embedded in it. And when she held it up so it could unfurl to its full length, she saw the bottom was flame, reds and yellows flaring up into the black.

She stared at it, lost for words.

"I'd like you to wear that when I take you to dinner," Cipher said from where he leaned against her door.

"On Corsica?" There were nice restaurants, but nothing where she'd need a gown. Space stations were prone to more practical attire.

"Come back to Vemion with me."

"Your home world?" She recalled him telling her to

contact them when they thought Bart might not betray her so swiftly. "Why? I thought—" She didn't know what she thought. She was a poor human mechanic, he was a dragon lord, there was obviously nothing between them.

But the dress was so much more than nothing.

Cipher pushed off the door and stalked into the room. "Will you trust me?"

Between one blink and the next, he seemed to be across the room, but it was possible Morgan's brain was short circuiting. "What?"

He held out his hand and a lick of flame appeared. "Put your hand in the flame. Pull it out when it hurts."

"What?" she repeated. But she stared at the fire in his palm, inexorably drawn to it. Her fingers tingled and she wanted to touch.

But it was fire. Fire burned.

So why did her dragon lord want her to touch it?

He wanted to prove something, obviously. And she was just curious enough to want to know.

Curious, but not completely reckless.

She poked a finger at the flame and quickly pulled it out. But all it did was tickle. She poked it a second time, slower, giving herself a chance to be singed.

Nothing.

Laughing in wonder, she rested her whole hand in the flame, letting it dance around her fingers until it looked like she was the one who had summoned it.

Then Cipher pulled his palm away, but the fire stayed in her hand.

She stared at it, afraid that if she stopped looking, it might flare out of control. Not that she could control it. It was fire. That was impossible.

But there was a whole ball of it sitting in her palm as if she'd summoned it.

"Take it back," she told Cipher, panic just starting to edge into her voice.

"It's yours now." He was calm, but there was something in his tone she couldn't interpret. "You control it."

She very much did *not*. Mind unable to fully comprehend what was happening and desperate to make the fire go away, she clapped her hands together, smothering it.

It tickled her hands and winked out.

"What was that all about?" she demanded. The beautiful dress had crumpled to the floor and Morgan swiped it up before something happened to it. She hung it on a hook in the wardrobe.

Cipher closed the final gap between them, and swept her up into his arms. "It means you're my mate."

And then he kissed her.

MORGAN SANK INTO THE KISS, her body going a bit limp. But Cipher was there to take care of that, keeping a tight hold, his whole body firm against her.

Very firm. His hips pressed forward and the outline of his cock teased her stomach.

The dress she was wearing made her feel even more naked now. It would only take a flick of his hand to fully expose her and sink into her.

Yes, please.

Cipher's insistent kisses set her on fire. But unlike the one he'd summoned, this one could heat her up. But never harm her. She was beginning to understand that, even as her mind still reeled from his confession.

What did he mean by mate?

He teased her lips apart and she parted for him,

welcoming his tongue in a sweeping caress. She could spend half her life kissing this man. Maybe all of it. Her heart knew what it wanted, and for the first time, she dared to dream that maybe this was real.

They were both completely in control now. Her body was making demands of its own, but that all came from the desire that Cipher summoned in her, the way he made her feel.

His kisses didn't let up. Desire pooled low in her belly and she moaned against him. Cipher's leg slipped between hers and she rubbed against his thigh, needing the friction. Her moan turned into a gasp as Cipher's hand brushed against her breast.

He broke away from her, just for a moment, his own chest heaving as he breathed hard. "Tell me yes."

"You need to learn how to ask," she teased, a smile pulling at her own lips. He was being all lordly, and though it was hot as sin, she wasn't going to let him stomp all over her.

His eyes danced with flame. "Please, tell me yes."

She wasn't sure that counted, but if he didn't touch her soon, she might actually die. "Yes."

That was all he needed. They were only steps from the bed and all the promise that lay there. Better than a boulder in a cave. But she had a feeling that anywhere would be good, so long as she was with Cipher.

"Take that off," he told her as he pulled his own

shirt off, revealing muscles she hadn't gotten a chance to properly appreciate before.

Her mouth watered and she stared as he stripped down, revealing more and more of himself with every layer.

He'd just shucked off his pants, leaving nothing but the small black briefs that cupped his erection. "Take it off or I rip it off," he warned.

She might have dared him. Maybe some other time, she would. But he'd just bought the dress for her and she didn't want to ruin it. She pulled it over her head and chucked it in the still open wardrobe.

Cipher had a hand on his briefs, and it froze when she stood naked before him. He groaned and closed his eyes. "Fuck," he moaned, the curse coming out like a prayer.

She felt powerful. If some other guy looked away the moment she stripped naked, she might have taken it the wrong way. But energy seemed to vibrate under Cipher's skin.

She stalked closer and laid her hand over Cipher's. "Take if off or I rip it off," she said. She couldn't match his tone, and she couldn't stop smiling. Delight coursed through her.

She wanted him so much it hurt, but it was so right that her heart wanted to explode with joy.

Cipher stripped that final layer, but before she could look her fill, he swept her up and laid her down on the bed. Her legs fell open, any sense of propriety long gone, if she'd ever had it in the first place. Cipher looked down at her as if he intended to savor every inch.

She'd never expected to be devoured by a dragon. Now she couldn't wait.

And he kept the promise in his eyes, kissing his way down her body, taking his time to taste her breasts until she writhed beneath him, her sex wet and needy. She wanted him inside of her, needed it more than she needed her next breath.

And when he shifted, she could feel just how hard he was. He needed it too.

But he was determined to torture her.

His head dipped between her thighs and his tongue swept a stripe along her sex, making her arch into him and call out his name as she dug her fingers into his hair.

Cipher's mouth closed over her clit and she gasped, her body tightened with pleasure, and he didn't let up. The wave built slowly, each lick and swirl of his tongue taking her higher and higher until she was trembling on the edge.

She arched against him, still needing more, still reveling in the feel of his tongue against hers. She could get used to this.

Or she might die from it.

So long as Cipher was right there with her, she didn't care.

Orgasm crashed through her, her body vibrating with it as she crested and came.

Her heart beat fast and she felt almost like she could float. But she was still empty, still yearned for Cipher. "More," she demanded. "I need you inside me."

And Cipher, her mate, her dragon lord, let himself be commanded. He loomed over her, all big and broad and hers.

Yes, Morgan would never get enough of this.

His cock teased her, the blunt head pressing inside until that first hint of fullness made her mad for more. And more he gave her, easing himself in until they were as joined as two bodies could be.

It was perfect. Right. Everything that Morgan could want.

And then Cipher moved.

She lost herself in the sensation, her body swiftly finding another peak and convulsing around him as he pumped into her. And still he gave her more. And more.

And more.

The pleasure sat at the edge of pain and she rode it as hard as she could, her mind nothing but sensation and Cipher. And when he stiffened and found his own climax, she joined him one last time before her body went limp, taking far too much.

She might actually die from this, she thought for just a moment. But what a way to go.

They came back to themselves, eventually. Sweat cooled. Her body began to ache in all the right places. And Cipher was right there beside her through it all.

Morgan wanted to drift off to sleep and call this a perfect day. But she'd just slept for fifteen hours. And she'd barely woken up before she and Cipher went back to bed. Sleep wasn't an option.

"What do you mean by mate?" It sounded like everything she'd ever wanted wrapped up in one word. She'd heard of mates, of course. But humans didn't have mates. They bumbled around until they found someone who'd be good enough and kept on plowing through life.

She'd always secretly wanted a mate, though. How could she resist it?

Cipher pulled her close and rested his forehead against hers. His expression had gone soft, his haughty, lordly reserve gone. Here he was just Cipher. Just hers. "You controlled my flame. It didn't harm you. That's how I'm sure. But I've been growing to know it since we first met."

"I don't—" She didn't even know how to finish the sentence. How was a woman supposed to act when a dragon lord appeared out of nowhere and handed her all of her dreams on a silver platter?

"Come back to Vemion with me," Cipher said when it was clear she didn't have more to say. "Stay for a month. Get to know me and all I am. All we could be. That's all I ask."

That was *all?*

But…

Morgan wasn't doing anything else. And she already knew one way she and Cipher were compatible.

She leaned forward and kissed him. When she pulled back, she was smiling. "Yes."

TWENTY-TWO

"NO. NOPE. ABSOLUTELY NOT." Morgan looked up. And up. And up. There was no way that was actually Cipher.

I'll keep you safe, his voice echoed in her head. He'd warned her he could do that, but it was still strange.

Strange but good.

She'd been on Vemion for a week already, and though she hadn't said anything, she'd already made up her mind. He'd have to kick her off the planet if he wanted her to leave. She wouldn't go willingly.

But a girl had to have her limits. And the prospect of riding a dragon while he flew was butting up against the edge of hers.

He was a magnificent beast, that was for sure. Really, any dragoness would be proud to have him as a mate.

Too bad for them that he was hers.

She must have been quiet for too long.

We don't have to do this today, Cipher said. She could feel his words rumbling in her chest, even though he said nothing out loud. *When you're ready.*

In the distance, she spotted a dragon swooping through the air in tight rolls. "You're not going to try anything like that, are you?" She thought she knew her mate well enough, but there was trust, and then there was climbing onto a dragon's back without a harness.

Not on the first outing.

"Cipher!" She flicked one of his scales, though he probably didn't feel a thing.

You are always safe with me, my mate.

And that was the truth. She already knew it down to her bones. Morgan took a deep breath and clambered up where she'd been told, getting onto Cipher's wide back and finding her seat. There was so much of him that she wondered if she'd even realize they were flying.

Hold on.

That was her only warning. He jumped into the air and she *definitely* knew they were flying. She had to lunge forward to grab onto part of him, but in only a matter of seconds they leveled out.

Still hanging on? her mate asked.

She wanted to shout back a snarky comment, but

the wind was in her hair, and excitement and glee burst through her. Slowly, she let go with one hand, the other continuing to clutch at Cipher. She flung her arm out and soaked in the air.

Then she tilted her head back and laughed.

Perfect.

EPILOGUE

ONE YEAR *Later*

"Calm down," Morgan told him, patting a gentle hand on his shoulder as she crossed to the wardrobe. "All will be well."

"Will it?" He was in a fine suit, kitted out like he was going for dinner with the king, rather than with his mother. Of course, facing Uncle Venin might be an easier prospect than this.

"If one of us should be nervous, it should be me," Morgan pointed out as she slipped into the gown he'd bought her on Corsica Station.

It wasn't the first time she'd worn it for him, but every time he saw her in it, she stole his breath. Though she didn't need to be wearing the gown to do that.

"My mother will..." He wanted to say that his

mother would love Morgan, but he couldn't make that promise. He knew his mother too well.

"You've had a year to prepare me for this, Cipher. If she finds me unacceptable, what will you do?" She fit amber earrings into her earlobes as she spoke.

"I shall keep you as a concubine while I find a proper wife," he answered promptly.

Morgan rolled her eyes and shot him a gesture which would prove to his mother that she was inappropriate. "You do that, and I'm sure I can find a different hunk of a dragon to shack up with," she teased.

It was a back and forth they'd had more than once, but still he growled and stalked towards his mate. "You're mine," he promised as he loomed over her.

Morgan grinned. "And if I'm unsuitable?"

"You're mine," he repeated.

She leaned in and kissed him quickly. "I love you too."

He wanted to take her there. For any other meeting, he might have. But his mother had been gone for her promised year and her ship was due to return within an hour. He and his mate needed to be at the dock to greet her.

And he wondered who she would choose. A year was a long time, and every day with his mate was a joy. But his mother would have never expected him to take a human.

And what would she think of Storm and Drake?

He shook his head. His brothers had to face his mother on their own.

He didn't know if she would name him as her heir and he no longer cared. No matter what, he had Morgan at his side. His brothers would always be his brothers, and he wouldn't let the inheritance tear them apart.

They just had to face the day.

His communicator beeped and he stood. "Our ride is here," he told Morgan, holding out a hand.

She laced her fingers with his. "Let's go."

Thank you for reading *Cipher*!
The series continues with Storm.

WHAT TO READ NEXT: STORM

He's not looking for a mate…

Dragon lord Storm is under an ultimatum: find a bride or lose his inheritance. But he is no man to be pushed around. When a matchmaker instructs him where to look for his mate, he's determined to refuse.

Unfortunately some orders must be followed. Especially when they come from the king. And when he sets eyes on River, a human woman from a diplomatic delegation, he's determined to make her his own.

It's a simple enough plan. Until an attack puts River, Storm, and two diplomatic delegations in danger. With only River to rely on, Storm will find exactly what his mate is made of.

But can he convince his strong and feisty human to rely on him and accept him as her mate?

INTERGALACTIC DATING AGENCY

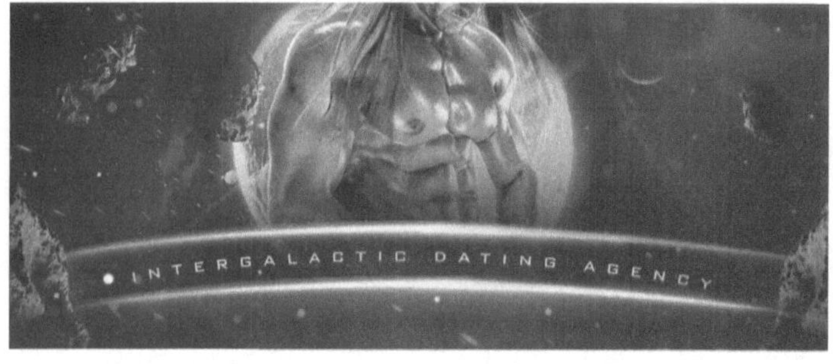

LOOKING for love that's out of this world? These strong, smart, sexy aliens are seeking mates from the Milky Way. Just hop onboard with your local Intergalactic Dating Agency. Join our group of authors as we explore the friendly skies and beyond with trilogies of cosmic craving, astral adventure, and otherworldly lovers. Warning: abductions may or may not be included!

ALSO BY KATE RUDOLPH

Looking for something else? Kate Rudolph has a heart pounding collection or paranormal and sci-fi romance stories for you! Bundles, bears, audiobooks, aliens, and more. Check out your options in the list below. You can find out all you need to know at www.katerudolph.net.

Want to check out one of the books? Click on the series name to find out more!

Dragon Brides

Fated mates, fierce women, and dragon princes.

Also available in audio!

Crux

Ranger

Saber

Cipher

Storm

Drake

———

Alien Mates: Planet Exile

Guerran is no place for pretty human women. But these alien heroes will protect their mates!

Also available in audio!

Exile's Hunter

Exile's Adored

————

Zulir Warrior Mates

Kidnapped humans. Alien Warriors. Electric wings.

The Zulir Warrior Mates series brings you human heroines and heroes abducted from Earth who find love – and wings! – with the alien warriors who rescue them.

Also available in audio!

Synnr's Saint

Synnr's Hope

Synnr's Spark

Synnr's Kiss

————

Guarded by the Shifter

Werewolf. Bodyguard. Mate.

The origins of these shifters are shrouded in mystery, but they're determined to protect their mates from any harm that comes their way.

Also available in audio!

Hunting Season

On the Prowl

Stalking Magic

Hungry for the Wolf

———

Detyen Warriors

Detya was destroyed a hundred years ago. These doomed warriors are out to find justice… and their mates.

The Detyen Warriors series brings you kick butt heroines, alpha alien heroes, fated mates, and relationships strong enough to span the galaxy!

The entire series is also available in audio!

Soulless

Ruthless

Heartless

Faultless

Endless

———

Alien Holiday Romance

Christmas… in space????

These alien holiday romances look beyond Earth's winter holidays and ring in the season across the galaxy! *Select titles available in audio.*

Snowed in with the Alien Beast

The Alien's Winter Gift

The Alien Reindeer's Wild Ride

Trapped with her Alien Mate

———

Alien Outlaws

Outlaws, schemes, and love… it's all there in the Alien Outlaws series…

Andie Munster is sick of life on Ixilta, the planet she got dumped on after being abducted from Earth six years ago. And when the mysterious and dangerous Xandr shows up looking for a way off the planet, she's half-prisoner, half-co-conspirator in a wild rush to escape.

Rogue Alien's Escape

Rogue Alien's Woman

Rogue Alien's Secret

Rogue Alien's Legacy

Mated to the Alien

Fated Mate Alien Romance

Detyens are doomed to die young if they don't find their fated mates.

Follow along as these mated pairs fight off aliens, corrupt dictators, prejudiced humans, pirates, and more! The books can be read or listened to in any order, though some characters show up in multiple stories.

Select books available in audio.

Pick a book and jump into the action today!

Ruwen

Tyral

Stoan

Cyborg

Krayter

Kayleb

Shayn

Braxtyn

Doryan

Dekon

Stealing the Alpha

The thief takes what she wants, but the alpha keeps what's his…

Join shifter thief Mel as she clashes with lion alpha Luke in an explosive trilogy of two opposites who can't keep away from one another.

Also available in audio!

The Alpha Heist

Entangled with the Thief

In the Alpha's Bed

Save with box sets!

Aliens. Shifters. Warriors. Mates. Get them all wrapped together in these special box sets. Save up to 30% off the price of buying the individual books, depending on the series!

Alien Outlaws: The Complete Series

Mated to the Alien Volume One (also available in audio)

Mated to the Alien Volume Two (also available in audio)

Mated to the Alien Volume Three

Mated to the Alien Volume Four

Stealing the Alpha: The Complete Series (also available in audio)

The Mate Bundle

Detyen Warriors Volume One (also available in audio)

Detyen Warriors Volume Two (also available in audio)

Zulir Warrior Mates Volume One (also available in audio)

Standalone Paranormal and Sci-Fi Romance:

Crashed

Mated on the Moon

Mated to the Alien Dragon

Marked

Bear in Mind

Alpha's Mercy

Gemma's Mate

Find more by Kate Rudolph at www.katerudolph.net

ABOUT KATE RUDOLPH

Kate Rudolph is a paranormal and alien romance author who lives in Indiana. She loves writing about kick butt heroines and the steamy heroes who love them. She's been devouring romance novels since she was too young to be reading them and had to hide her books so no one would take them away. She couldn't imagine a better job in this world than writing romances and sharing them with her fellow readers.

If you enjoyed this story, please consider leaving a review.